PSYCHIC ZONE

THE ENEMY WITHIN

MATHEW STONE

Hodder
Children's
Books

a division of Hodder Headline plc

Copyright © 1998 Mathew Stone

First published in Great Britain in 1998
by Hodder Children's Books

The right of Nigel Robinson to be identified as the Author of
the Work has been asserted by him in accordance with the
Copyright, Designs and Patents Act 1988.

10 9 8 7 6 5 4 3 2 1

A Catalogue record for this book is available from
the British Library

ISBN 0 340 69838 1

Typeset by Avon Dataset Ltd, Bidford-on-Avon, Warks

Printed and bound in Great Britain by
Clays Ltd, St Ives plc

Hodder Children's Books
A Division of Hodder Headline plc
338 Euston Road
London NW1 3BH

CONTENTS

THE PSYCHIC ZONE

Prologue

Three Months to Earth

Dateline: Mission Control, Houston, Texas;
Thursday 26 March; 15.16.

Morgan Knight looked up apprehensively at the row
of screens in front of her in Mission Control Centre.
Some of them displayed aerial views of the entire
globe, the familiar landmasses crisscrossed by flight
paths and moving dots which indicated the various
paths of hundreds of satellites continuing their
interminable orbits of planet Earth. Other screens
scrolled up rows upon rows of calculations and
notations which Morgan vaguely recognised from
high school. Sitting in front of them were several
white-coated scientists and technicians, assiduously
taking down notes on their clipboards and discussing
with each other the views presented on the screen.

They weren't what Morgan was interested in, and

neither were the pictures of the Earth taken from almost a hundred and fifty million kilometres out in space. There was only one screen which held Morgan's entire attention. That was the one showing the figure of the spacesuited astronaut as he effected repairs to the *Deimos III* spacecraft, floating in the sub-zero blackness of space.

In the background, hanging just over the astronaut's shoulder, she could make out the rusty-brown sphere of a planet: the planet Mars. The *Deimos III* was the third in a series of exploratory craft sent out to pave the way for the first manned mission to Mars, which was scheduled for a couple of years' time.

The astronaut was Armstrong Knight, Morgan's father.

Still keeping her eyes firmly fixed on her dad, Morgan walked over to one of the command consoles which were lined up in neat rows in front of the banks of monitoring equipment. One of the white-coated technicians smiled at her, flipped a switch, and swung the microphone in her direction.

Morgan bent down over the microphone. 'Hi, Dad, it's me,' she said. 'You're looking fine.' There was a momentary pause as the radio waves took their time to cross the hundred and fifty million kilometres which separated Armstrong Knight from his only daughter. Then there came a crackling sound and Armstrong's voice hissed over the PA system.

'Morgan? That you?'

Armstrong's voice sounded a little indistinct. That was only to be expected, the NASA scientists had warned Morgan. There was some higher than usual sunspot activity at the moment, which was interfering with their radio communications. It was the influence of those sunspots which had interfered with the *Deimos III's* navigational equipment in the first place, requiring Armstrong to take his spacewalk and make the necessary repairs.

''Course it's me,' came back Morgan's cheery reply. 'Who else'd be ringing you up all the way from little old planet Earth?'

She heard her father chuckle, and he turned his face towards the on-board video camera which was recording his every move. He couldn't see Morgan, of course, although she liked to think that he could.

'Sure do miss the old place,' he said. Armstrong and his three other fellow astronauts on-board the *Deimos* had been in space for over three months now. It would be at least another three before they would return to the Earth. 'And I miss you, too, Morgan . . .'

Morgan swallowed the lump in her throat. All around the world millions of others also felt a lump in their throats. The Knights' conversation was being broadcast simultaneously on the CNN network and BBC Worldwide, in a PR move to generate some public interest (as well as ready cash) in the increasingly unpopular space program. That was why Morgan had been allowed to talk to her dad on the vital satellite link between Earth and space.

Morgan took her glasses off, a familiar habit

whenever she was feeling awkward or embarrassed. 'I miss you too, Dad. And I'm real proud of you.'

Morgan waited for the customary delay for her dad's reply to reach Earth. It never came. Morgan looked at the technician standing by the microphone.

'What's up?' There was a hint of nervousness in her voice.

'It's OK,' he said coolly, as though there was nothing wrong at all. 'Probably just some more sunspot interference. I'll re-align the transceivers.' He calmly twiddled a few old-fashioned-looking knobs on the console and jabbed at a few keypads.

'–ward to seeing you soon.' Armstrong Knight's voice returned, and Morgan breathed a sigh of relief.

She knew that there had been nothing wrong. It had simply been the audio link that had gone down, and not the video link. She could still see her dad floating around on the outside of the *Deimos III*. She was just being nervy.

But then, being nervy had always been Morgan Knight's problem. She wished she could be as level-headed and sophisticated as the worldly-wise Liv Farrar. Morgan sure was glad that Liv was going to be around when she made use of that generous scholarship to attend that fancy Institute place way over in the UK. At least she knew that she would have a friend there.

'It was real weird not having you around for Christmas Day,' said Morgan. Neither of the Armstrongs was religious, but they still liked getting together with the rest of their family for an afternoon of turkey and cranberry sauce. And watching reruns of classic films on the tube.

'I'll make up for it when–'

The audio link cut out again and, when it returned, Armstrong's voice was much fainter. It now seemed further away, further away even than the halfway point to Mars. Morgan peered closer at her dad's image and frowned at the lines of static which started to streak across the video screen.

'Say, now is that real strange or what?' Armstrong's faraway voice came over the PA system. 'I've never seen anything like . . .'

'Dad? What is it?' Morgan asked. She strained to hear her dad's words above the crackle of static. To her horror, the picture on the screen slowly started to break up. 'What's wrong? What's happening?'

The interference on the audio link was getting stronger by the second and it was becoming more and more difficult to make out her father's words. The image on the screen started to slip and fall over and over itself.

'Don't know . . . it's like a whole . . . never seen anythi–'

The audio link fell. The picture on the screen blanked out.

The whole of Mission Control was thrown into a turmoil as the scientists and technicians struggled to restore the link. Morgan grabbed the arm of the technician next to her.

'What's going on?' she demanded urgently. 'What's happening to my dad?'

The technician glanced frantically at a series of LED read-outs which were displayed on the control console before him. He shook his head.

'I don't understand,' he said. 'All systems have crashed.'

'*All* systems?' Morgan asked.

'We've lost all contact with the *Deimos III*,' he told her, without looking at her.

His fingers flashed over the controls, trying to re-establish communications. All around him, people were doing the same. Even amongst these well-trained and experienced professionals, the tension was almost palpable. Most of the *Deimos III*'s life-support system was controlled by computer from Earth. If they couldn't reboot the system, then the on-board manual override would only remain functioning for a month at the most. The return trip to Earth was three months.

'You have to do something!' Morgan insisted. She was getting close to hysteria now. The technician turned angrily to her.

'And don't you think that we're trying all we can?' he said, before returning to his work. 'Now calm down or get out!'

Morgan shut up. She knew that all her shouting wouldn't help matters in the slightest. She forced herself to calm down.

Long anxious minutes passed. They seemed like years to Morgan. She knew that millions across the globe were sharing her distress, watching on CNN and BBC Worldwide. Somehow, that didn't help her in the slightest.

Mission Control was in silence, apart from the frantic click-click-clacking of fingers on keyboards and a few shouted orders to try that program or to delete that operation. The screen which had showed the outside of the *Deimos III* spacecraft remained blank.

Morgan tapped her foot in impatience and worry. She wished she believed in God or some other higher power. Then she would send Him a prayer. She did it anyway and, a short while later, it seemed that her prayer had been answered.

'. . . back to *Deimos*,' her dad's voice crackled over the loudspeaker. An image faded into view on the screen: Armstrong Knight making his slow way along the hull of the *Deimos III* and back towards the airlock, where his fellow astronauts would be waiting for him.

'Dad! You're OK!' Morgan breathed a sigh of relief.

''Course I'm safe,' Armstrong said, his voice clearer and louder now. Even the picture on the video screen seemed sharper and better defined. 'What's the hassle with you guys down there?'

'All the systems crashed,' Morgan said. 'Audio, visual, everything.'

'Not from our end, Honey,' Armstrong said. 'Everything's been working perfectly up here.'

Morgan glanced briefly at the technician beside her. Was that possible?

'Say, you really *were* worried, weren't you?' Armstrong said, as Morgan watched him activate the opening mechanism.

'Yeah.'

'There's no need to be, Honey,' Armstrong said

reassuringly. 'Everything is going perfectly fine.'

'I just thought that something else had gone wrong with the flight,' Morgan said. 'The mission hasn't gone smoothly since day one – or rather day twenty.'

Up in space, Armstrong Knight smiled. *Deimos III* had been due to blast off for Mars on the first day of December. It had been delayed by twenty days because one of the technicians on the project had decided that conditions hadn't been quite right. Several people had queried her decision but, in the end, she had had her way, producing a print-out of facts and figures which seemed to prove her judgement right.

'Now don't worry, Honey, everything's going to be perfect from now on,' he said. He clicked off his communication link with Mission Control.

Morgan was so relieved that her dad was safe, she didn't even think to ask him what it was that he had mentioned seeing just before the audio and visual links cut out.

In fact, she only mentioned it to him three months later, after he'd returned to Earth and when she was making preparations to go over to Europe to study at the Institute. He didn't reply.

Because by then it was much, much too late.

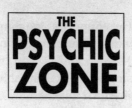

THE PSYCHIC ZONE

1

New Arrivals

*Dateline: Junior Common Room,
The Brentmouth Institute for Scientifically
Gifted Youngsters; Tuesday 12 January; 13.30.*

'Marc Price, I do believe that you are in *lurrve!*'

The tall blonde-haired boy in the leather jacket grimaced and chomped down on his second hamburger with double cheese and bacon. Tomato ketchup dribbled down his chin and stained the front of his T-shirt, which advertised the latest heavy metal band. Rebecca Storm didn't know which was worse: Marc's eating habits, or the fact that he was behaving more like some love-struck kid than the highly intelligent science student he really was.

Marc narrowed his eyes and glowered at Rebecca. 'Am not,' he said, sounding like a little kid whose dad had just spotted him doing something particularly embarrassing. He wiped the ketchup from his lips with a paper napkin and reached out for another onion ring.

'Then how come you've talked about nothing else but Morgan Knight for the past week?' asked Joey Williams. Joey was a streetsmart and sassy black kid from New York's Harlem district, and there was nothing he liked better than joining up with Rebecca in some good-natured teasing of Marc.

'You and half the male population of the Institute,' Rebecca said.

'You jealous, Bec?' Marc asked wickedly, determined to get his own back on Rebecca as well as change the subject.

'Dream on.'

Marc and Joey exchanged a knowing look. They weren't fooled for a second. There was definitely a trace of resentment in Rebecca's voice. With her long auburn hair, trim figure, and quick and ready personality, Rebecca had long secretly enjoyed being regarded as one of the best-looking girls at the Brentmouth Institute for Scientifically Gifted Youngsters – until Morgan Knight had joined the school one week ago for the start of the Spring Term, that was.

Next to Morgan Knight, every other girl in the school might as well have considered signing up for the role of one of the three witches in *Macbeth*, so sophisticated and attractive was the newcomer. Even Liv Farrar had been surprised by Morgan's transformation from the gawky fourteen-year-old she'd met on one of her study trips to the US, to sexy blonde bombshell.

Morgan had already caught the appreciative eye of every male student from the young kids right up to the smoothies of the Upper Sixth. Even Mr Rutherford, the senior chemistry lecturer, had broken one of his unwritten laws and given her an A for her very first piece of work for him.

'I've got better things to worry about than boys,' Rebecca said haughtily, and tossed back her hair the way she always did when she wasn't quite telling the truth. She looked at the two empty hamburger cartons in front of Marc and decided that it was her turn to change the subject.

'Have you never heard of healthy eating?' she asked, clearly unimpressed by the amount that Marc had consumed for his lunch.

'No,' Marc said happily, and burped for effect.

Rebecca smiled wryly. No matter how much Marc ate, he never put a pound on his wiry figure. Bec, on the other hand, carefully watched what she ate in order to maintain her figure. Maybe she ought to start visiting the Institute gym, too, she wondered, even if it was just to compete with Morgan Knight. (Not that she was jealous, of course.).

'You should try one, Rebecca,' Joey said. He had just finished off a lamb-burger with mint sauce and chives. 'These new school caterers are just the limit.'

Rebecca pulled a face. She was a vegetarian and there seemed to be nothing on the new school canteen menu which appealed to her. 'I wish Mrs Chapman were still here,' Rebecca said. 'She might have fed you meat-eaters on a steady diet of stodge and grease, but at least she looked out for us veggies.'

'Funny about the old bird suddenly just packing up and going like that,' said Marc, who had always had a soft spot for the cheery-faced dinner lady. 'She'd been at the Institute for ages.'

'Well, of course, you know who was behind all that, don't you?' asked Joey.

'No,' replied Marc. 'Who?'

'Like, I got bored at the beginning of term and thought I'd do some studying in the library,' he said, and was disappointed when neither Rebecca nor Marc appeared to believe him. 'So, I was passing Axford's office, right?'

'Which is nowhere near the library,' Rebecca pointed out. In fact, the Institute library and the Principal's office were in two different buildings. 'Admit it, Joey, you were snooping around.'

Joey bowed his head. 'OK, so I figured that there'd be no one in the staff-room and that maybe I could sneak in and see if Smethurst had left the papers to next week's math paper lying around. You know how forgetful he is . . .'

'That's cheating, Joey,' Rebecca reproved, with a smile. Joey ignored her.

'Anyways, I was passing Axford's office, and the door was open, and I heard Eva agreeing terms on the phone with the new caterers.'

'Eva. Why is it that she seems to be behind

everything that happens at the Institute?' Marc asked, rhetorically.

Eva was the personal assistant of General Axford, a tall and steely-eyed blonde in dark glasses, who everyone at the Institute held in frightened awe. Even General Axford himself seemed always to defer to his assistant's decisions.

'I'm surprised that the catering arrangements here at the Institute interest her,' Rebecca said.

'*Everything* at the Institute interests Eva,' Marc remarked.

'Even so, I wouldn't have expected providing you carnivores with hamburgers and lamb steaks to be high on her list of priorities,' Rebecca said. 'I don't think I've ever seen her eat *anything* – let alone meat – in my life.'

'Bet she still loves the sight of blood,' Marc said, and didn't have to explain what he meant. None of them had any concrete proof, of course, but they were all by now pretty certain that Eva was a member of the Project, a top-secret organisation whose evil influence stretched all across the globe.

'Ah, well, that's down to Morgan Knight, isn't it?' Joey said knowledgeably.

'It would be,' Rebecca replied huffily, starting to wish that she'd never brought the subject up in the first place. Still, she was intrigued. 'Why does it all come down to Morgan Knight?'

'From what I hear, Morgan's old man wasn't too impressed with the prospectus Axford sent out to him,' Joey continued, and was interrupted by Marc.

'That's crazy: the Institute is one of the best science schools in the country – the world even,' he said. 'Everyone wants to send their kids here: high-flying government ministers, minor royalty, sons and daughters of billionaire businessmen and women . . .'

'Sure,' Joey acknowledged. He knew he'd been really lucky winning a scholarship to Brentmouth. It had been the only chance a slum kid like him had to get away from the dead-end future that faced him back in New York. 'But it seems Morgan's dad didn't like the idea of her eating Chapman's slop in the canteen all the time. He wasn't too sold on the on-site accommodation that Axford offered them either, come to think of it.'

'I know,' Rebecca said. She remembered what their friend from Brentmouth village, Colette Russell, had told them earlier that week. 'She's moved into a small private cottage in the village with some creepy housekeeper.'

'You mean Morgan's dad insisted that the catering arrangements here should be changed?' Marc asked. 'All so's his daughter wouldn't have to eat Ma Chapman's meat and two veg for lunch?'

'Something like that,' Joey replied. 'He offered to pay for most of the change himself.'

'Then the guy must have more money than sense,' Rebecca said, with a twinge of envy. It had been hard going for her Mom and herself ever since her dad, Nathan, had died in that weird accident a while back. But recently, her mom had been experiencing even more financial troubles, to such an extent that her tuition fees for this term still hadn't been paid. 'Maybe going all the way to Mars and back affected his brain!'

Joey grinned. 'Still, I sure ain't got no complaints. That pastrami-on-rye I had for lunch yesterday was one of the best I've ever had since I left New York! Correction: I never tasted anything like it before!'

'*Puh-leease*,' Rebecca scoffed, and felt her stomach turn at the thought of the meat. 'Sure, Armstrong Knight is one of the most famous guys on the planet at the moment, but then he *is* an astronaut.'

'And an astronaut who's come within eighty million kilometres of Mars,' Marc reminded her. 'That's closer than any other human being has ever been before. Think of the things he might have seen out there.'

'A dead planet, way smaller than Earth, and with an atmosphere that's been incapable of supporting any sort of life for aeons? Like, I'm supposed to be impressed?' she asked sarcastically, and then smiled as she realised that both Marc and Joey knew exactly just how impressed she really was.

'*And* a millionaire several times over, who's promised to pump some of his well-earned bread into the Institute,' Joey finished. 'Is it any wonder that Eva and Axford agreed to let him demand that the catering arrangements be changed *and* pay off Ma Chapman with a mega-retirement sum?'

Rebecca considered the matter for a moment. She knew that, even with its sizeable annual government grant from the Ministry of Technocratic Planning and Development, the Institute still depended to an appreciable extent on generous outside donations.

'I guess you're right,' she finally admitted. 'There's nothing which matters more to General Axford and Eva than the future well-being of their Institute. Sometimes it's like an obsession. Still, there's one thing that's sort of bothering me.'

'Like what?' asked Joey. 'Like how someone such as Marc thinks he even has a chance with Morgan Knight when someone as sexy and as cool as Yours Truly is around?'

'No,' replied Rebecca with a smile. 'How did Armstrong Knight become a millionaire so quickly? I mean, the salary of someone working for NASA – even way up in Martian space – isn't exactly in the multi-millionaire league.'

'Who cares?' Joey shrugged and reached out for one of Marc's onion rings. Marc snatched the cardboard carton away from him.

'Sorry, Joey,' he said, and wolfed the two remaining rings down. 'You want food: you pay for it!' Marc grinned at them. 'I'll see you two later,' he announced. 'I've got work to do.'

'No you haven't,' Rebecca said, and glanced at her watch. 'You've got a free period until three o'clock.'

'Not that sort of work,' Marc replied. 'I've got a job to do for *The Enquirer*.'

Forgetting Marc's earlier slight, Joey grinned. 'Hey, way to go, big buddy,' he said. 'So you finally persuaded Liv Farrar to let you work alongside her?' It was an open secret at the Institute that Marc had fancied the attractive editor of the school newspaper for quite some time. Up till now, she had made a point of ignoring him totally.

'Sure,' Marc said, and his chest swelled with pride. 'And guess what assignment she's given me?'

'Surprise us,' challenged Rebecca.

'Interviewing Morgan Knight, no less!'

'We see her in classes every day,' Rebecca remarked, a little jealously. 'What's so special about her?'

'Liv just thinks that there's so much interest in Morgan's dad and his experiences in space that it'd be a good idea to talk to Morgan about him,' Marc replied. 'That way, Morgan won't be bothered by any creeps pestering her throughout the term.'

Joey let out a whistle of appreciation. 'You sly mutha, you!' he said admiringly. 'Alone in a room with Morgan Knight! It's the dream of every red-blooded male from here to Kansas City!'

Rebecca let out a long and heartfelt sigh. 'Honestly!' she implored. 'You two guys are the worst examples I've ever seen of hormonally-challenged and testosterone-overloaded male libido ever!'

'Huh?' asked Marc.

'You're both obsessed with sex!' Rebecca said, with a superior snigger.

She stood up to go; unlike Marc, she had a physics class at two and she didn't want to be late. As she made her way towards the door of the Junior Common Room, it opened and a smartly dressed Chinese-looking boy entered, carrying a folder stuffed full of papers. He looked around the room, spotted Marc, Rebecca and Joey, and went over to them.

'Hi, Johnny,' Rebecca said. The fourteen-year-old's name was, in fact, Lau Teng Lee, but he liked to be known as Johnny. He nodded a brief welcome to each of them and then looked enquiringly at Marc.

'Are you ready, Marc?' he asked. Johnny's English was clear and precise and with hardly any trace of an accent.

Marc frowned. 'Ready for what?' he asked.

Johnny's face fell and he indicated the folder he was carrying under his arm. 'You told me that you had a free period,' he reminded him. 'You promised you'd help me out with my biology holiday assignment.'

'I did?' Marc asked absently, pretending that he'd forgotten. 'It can wait, can't it?'

Johnny shook his head. 'I was supposed to complete it by the beginning of term,' he reminded him. 'General Axford said that I could have another week to finish it. I have to hand it in by Thursday morning, at the latest.'

Marc let out an exaggerated yawn. 'Look, Johnny, it's going to have to wait,' he said.

Johnny's face fell. 'But you promised . . .' he said, his voice full of disappointment.

'Just as you promised Axford that you'd deliver by the beginning of term,' Marc pointed out, and glanced at his Swatch. 'I'll see what I can do later, OK? For the moment I've got far more important things to do than help people who couldn't be bothered to finish their homework on time!'

And with that, Marc left the Junior Common Room. Johnny turned disconsolately to Rebecca and Joey.

'He promised,' he said miserably.

'I'm sorry, Johnny,' Rebecca apologised on behalf of Marc, and then added sarcastically: 'Like the typical male he is, he's only got one thing on his mind right now.'

'It should be a matter of honour,' Johnny said. 'In my land, when we make a promise, then we keep that promise.'

'And so does Marc normally,' Rebecca said, and then smiled sympathetically. 'I'll have a word with him about it later. I'm sure he'll help you out before you get into trouble with General Axford.'

''Course, if you'd've kept *your* promise to Axford then this wouldn't've happened, would it?' Joey said.

Rebecca looked strangely at Joey. There was a tone in his voice which she'd never heard before. 'What d'you mean, Joey?' she asked.

'Well, if Johnny here had delivered his work on time, he wouldn't have had to come running to Marc,' Joey said.

'I seem to remember you ringing me up over the vacation to ask for some help on your math assignment,' Rebecca recalled.

'Yeah, but that's different,' Joey replied.

'I don't see how,' Rebecca said, a little frostily, and then turned back to Johnny. 'Still, Joey is right, y'know, Johnny. How come you didn't finish your stuff in time?

Johnny turned away guiltily, as though he didn't want to meet Rebecca and Joey's eyes. 'There were – matters to attend to at home . . .' he said evasively, and when Rebecca and Joey pressed him a little further, he added: 'Problems with my family . . .'

'Families can be a real pain sometimes, can't they?' Rebecca agreed sympathetically. She thought of her dad. She wished he were alive now. And everytime she'd tried to talk to Marc about it recently, he'd gone and changed the subject.

Johnny looked down at his folder and sighed. 'Then, if Marc cannot help me, I must try and see if I can finish the work myself,' he said.

'Like you should've done in the first place,' Joey said, uncharitably.

'Joey!' Rebecca reproved, but Johnny nodded his head in agreement.

'No, Rebecca,' he said meekly, 'Joey is right. I should have made time during the holidays to complete my assignment.'

'Well, yeah, sure, but if you had family problems,' Rebecca said. 'I'm sure General Axford would understand . . .'

Johnny smiled, knowing – just as Rebecca knew – that, when it came to families, the stern-hearted Principal of the Institute understood nothing. He bade both of them goodbye and left the common room. As soon as he had gone, Rebecca turned to Joey.

'Joey! How could you!' she said. 'You were being really nasty to Johnny, just then. That's not like you at all.'

Joey rammed his hands in the pockets of his jeans and sulked. 'Maybe not,' he admitted, a little begrudgingly. 'But there's something about that guy I don't like.'

'Such as?' As far as Rebecca was concerned, Johnny Lau was a nice enough kid, always polite and a hard worker, if at times a little too nice for his own good.

'Just a feeling, that's all,' he said. 'Like he's hiding something from us. Colette thinks the same as well. She told me as much the other day when I was down at Fiveways.'

Rebecca was interested now. Both Joey and Colette possessed certain psychic talents, the existence of which many scientists were, even now, reluctant to consider. And, although Joey's abilities were far stronger than Colette's, Colette Russell still had an understanding of people's true nature that was almost uncanny. If Colette said that someone wasn't quite as they seemed, then she was very probably right.

'She thinks that he's some kind of impostor?' she asked.

'I didn't say that,' Joey corrected her. 'But there's more to him than meets the eye. Why else would Axford be taking his biology classes?'

'The General is a qualified biologist as well as an ex-military man,' Rebecca said. 'Why shouldn't he?'

'For the past few years, General Axford has devoted all his time to running the Institute with Eva,' Joey continued. 'Why should he suddenly show such a special interest in Johnny Lau and take up teaching again?'

'Could be that he misses it?' Rebecca replied, not at all unreasonably. 'Working alongside the Ice Queen every hour of the day would make biology with Year Eight seem like heaven!'

Joey chuckled and then his voice became grimmer.

'Besides, you never can trust these Chinese, can you?'

Rebecca frowned. She asked Joey to explain.

'Well, like, they're kind a different to you and me, aren't they?' he said casually. 'I mean, they don't even look the same. And then they come over to *our* Institute from their own country and get special treatment from Axford. Believe me, Rebecca, you just can't trust people like that. Everyone knows that.'

Rebecca bit her lip to control the anger which she could feel welling up inside her. What Joey was saying was so close to racism that she couldn't quite believe what she was hearing.

'Johnny Lau got here through his own merits just like everyone else,' she protested.

'Yeah?' Joey said, and now there was no mistaking the scorn in his voice. 'Then how come he never gets a grade higher than a D in all the time he's been at the Institute?'

This was news to Rebecca. An occasional D, or even an E, was not unheard of at the Institute, but they were the very rare exceptions rather than the rule.

'How do you know that?' she demanded.

'I told you, I sneaked into the staff-room the other day,' he replied. 'Someone had left the results of December's exams on one of the tables. I tell you, Rebecca, someone like Johnny oughta be sent back all the way back to China or wherever it is that he comes from. His kind are out of place at the

Institute. He sure as hell don't belong here with us!'

Rebecca regarded Joey through accusing eyes. 'I bet that's what some people said about you too, you know,' she said pointedly.

'Whaddya mean?'

'A black kid from New York, attending one of the top schools in the world,' she said. 'What right have you got to take the place of some white kid from, say, the Glasgow slums? Maybe it would have been better if you'd stayed back in Harlem. At least you'd be with your own kind there.'

Joey glared at Rebecca. 'You don't mean that,' he said, as he clenched and unclenched his fists in anger.

'No, of course I don't,' Rebecca reassured him, and Joey calmed down. 'You got here on your own merits – just like Marc and I did, and just like Johnny as well. Just like we *all* did.'

Joey frowned and a shudder seemed to pass through his body. It was if he was realising for the first time just exactly what it was that he had said. He raised a hand to his brow.

'I don't believe I just said what I did.'

'Neither do I,' Rebecca agreed.

'You were right,' he said. 'Some of the scumbags back home said that I was a no-good nigger who didn't deserve to come here. I shouldn't have been so mean about Johnny.'

'Maybe you should apologise to him?' Rebecca suggested.

Joey paused for a half-instant and then said, 'Yeah,

sure I will. Say, I can help him out with his biology assignment to make up for being such a scuzzball just then.'

'You will be helping no one with any assignment, Mr Williams,' came a clipped voice, that was as cold as the bitter January wind lashing the branches of the yew trees against the windows outside.

Joey and Rebecca looked up. Eva was standing before them, dressed, as usual, in her black power-suit and her dark glasses that she never, ever, removed. Several other students in the common room looked warily at her. By rights, none of the teaching staff was allowed in the Junior Common Room. But then, Eva was no teacher and, even if she had have been, she would still have broken the rule.

'Joey was only suggesting that he could help Johnny Lau with his biology assignment,' Rebecca said, wondering just how Eva could always stalk up on them so silently. Sometimes it was almost as if she could appear out of thin air.

'Each student at our Institute must do his or her own work,' Eva stated, in a emotionless monotone.

'I was trying to be friendly, that's all,' Joey said. *Not that someone like you would know what friendship is*, he thought. Not once had he seen Eva help another human being.

Eva regarded Joey through her dark glasses and he shuddered. There were some times when Joey thought that she wasn't even quite human. There was no way that he could ever bring himself to trust her.

'You will not assist Lau Teng Lee any more,' Eva declared.

'Why not?' Rebecca asked, and returned Eva's frosty stare. She was determined not to let herself be intimidated by Eva, the way Joey had been. 'What's wrong with helping each other out?'

Eva now turned her attention to Rebecca and, despite herself, Rebecca felt the same shudder through her body that Joey had experienced.

'Apart from attendance at classes, neither of you will associate with Lau Teng Lee again. Is that understood?' Eva said. This was too much for Rebecca and she felt the anger rise inside her again.

'Why?' she demanded.

'*Never again*,' Eva repeated, making it clear that she had no intention whatsoever of answering Rebecca's question. Then she added menacingly: 'and, if you disobey, then you may find that your scholarships to the Institute will be revoked.'

With that final threat, Eva left Rebecca and Joey and marched over to the student noticeboard at the far end of the common room. She cast her eyes over the usual posters and notices pinned up there.

There were drugs awareness leaflets and charity flyers, exam timetables and ads for an overpriced gig by the latest indie band. Several posters advertised the Institute's special-interest groups such as the Astronomy Club and the Folklore and Anthropology Society. There were also notices promoting one or other of the Institute's several religious groups, including one garishly coloured poster for an organisation called the New Dawn.

Eva ignored all of these and finally found the notice she was looking for. She snorted with contempt and then ripped it off the board, scrunched it into a ball, and tossed it into a bin.

After Eva had left the common room, Rebecca and Joey walked over to the wastepaper bin, where Rebecca bent down and fished out the notice Eva had disposed of.

'So what's the big deal?' Joey asked, as Rebecca started to smooth out the piece of paper. He glanced idly at one of the posters on the board: *The New Dawn: A New Order for the New Millennium*, it read. 'What's upset the Ice Queen this time?'

'This,' said Rebecca. She handed Joey the piece of paper, which he recognised instantly. It was a flyer urging local people and students from the Institute to attend a public demonstration in a few days' time.

'It's that eco-gig that Colette's involved with,' he realised, as he scanned the details of the poster.

Zhou-zhun, one of the newly-powerful and independent Asian nations had finally decided to come clean about the nuclear weapons in their possession. They were ready to give them all up, as long as a suitable site could be found to dump their deadly load of plutonium.

In a controversial move, the British Government had agreed to dispose of several of these nuclear missiles off Penwyn-Mar on the south-west coast. The convoy of lorries carrying the missiles was scheduled to pass by the Institute in a matter of days' time, *en route* for the coast.

Not surprisingly there was a lot of local opposition along the entire length of the route. Even though Colette wasn't a student at the Institute, she had joined a sizeable proportion of the school's students in opposing the operation.

'Why doesn't Eva want this poster up here?' Rebecca said, and took the paper from Joey.

'Maybe she doesn't agree with what Colette and her buddies are planning on doing?' Joey suggested, although he knew that there was probably much more to it than that. With Eva, nothing was ever as simple as it appeared.

'She doesn't agree with lots of other things on the board as well,' Rebecca said, and drew his attention to the pop promos. Eva hated modern music. Eva seemed to hate everything which brought a smile to the faces of the people studying at the Institute. 'She doesn't tear those down, does she?'

'Maybe she *wants* the nuke to pass through Brentmouth?' Joey wondered, and then chuckled. 'Maybe she wants to hijack it. Imagine that! Eva with her hands on the trigger of a bunch of nuclear missiles!'

'That's not funny,' Rebecca said. She turned as she heard her name being called out: one of her fellow students was approaching her.

The newcomer was a tall, dreadlocked, and kindly-faced physics student from the year above Rebecca. He was dressed in a long, grungy sweater on to which he had pinned a variety of eco and peace badges and buttons. There was a ring in the side of his nose and several more along the lobe of his right ear. He smiled at Rebecca and Joey and then reached out his hand for the flyer which Rebecca had retrieved from the bin.

'I'll take that, Bec,' he said. His voice still carried the sing-song traces of a Welsh accent, even though his father was a multi-millionaire, who had sent his only son to a variety of top international schools before paying for his tuition fees at the Institute. Rebecca handed him the crumpled poster.

'Guess Eva isn't too keen on your and Colette's demonstration then, Griff?' Rebecca asked. She smiled: Griff was one of the nicest guys she'd ever met, always supporting half-a-dozen or more good causes, often to the detriment of his school-work, and with never a bad or malicious word to say about anyone. She watched as he pinned the poster back on to the noticeboard.

'Tough,' Griff said, with uncharacteristic abruptness. 'Stopping this nuke from passing through the village is more important than whatever Eva wants.'

'It'll be OK,' Joey said. 'The government wouldn't let it pass through here if there were any sort of danger. It's bound to be safe.'

'That's what they said about Chernobyl too,' Griff said, and stood back to look at his handiwork. His poster slightly overlapped with the one advertising the group called the New Dawn. He wondered who they were: he'd certainly never heard of them before.

'Well, good luck,' Rebecca said encouragingly, and

then added a little mischievously: 'I'll give you a good couple of hours before Eva comes in here and tears down your poster again!'

Griff turned to address Rebecca and there was a strange, almost cold, look in his eyes which neither Rebecca nor Joey had ever seen before.

'She mustn't be allowed to do that,' he said. 'And, if she does try, then she shall have to be stopped.'

'Oh yeah?' Joey asked, lightly. 'You and whose army? Persuading Eva to do something she doesn't want to do is impossible!'

'Then she shall have to be killed,' Griff said with a smile, and left the room.

For a moment, neither Rebecca nor Joey knew whether he was serious or not. Then they both realised that Griff had to be joking.

He had to be, hadn't he?

After all, Griff wasn't like that at all.

Was he?

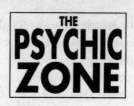
THE PSYCHIC ZONE

2

The New Dawn

Dateline: Fetch House, Brentmouth Village; Tuesday 12 January; 14.48.

Ever since she had arrived in England, Morgan Knight had been staying at Fetch House, a small chintzy cottage on a tiny hill overlooking Brentmouth village, and about a forty-five minute walk away from the Institute. Before Morgan had taken up residence here, the house had been used to put up scientists who were visiting or working at the nearby Fetch Hill radio-telescope.

As Marc was ushered into the tiny sitting-room by the housekeeper, a thirty-something dour-faced and tight-lipped woman called Miss Radclyffe, he wondered why Armstrong Knight had arranged for his daughter to stay here. Surely someone as glamorous and as sophisticated as Morgan Knight would have preferred staying at the girls' hostel in the Institute grounds, with its access to the Internet, PCs in every study bedroom, and cable TV – not to mention its proximity to the boys' hostel?

The only good thing about Fetch House seemed to be its location. It offered a panoramic view of the surrounding countryside: the Fetch Hill radio-telescope to the north, the Institute and Saint Michael's church to the west, and, coming from the east, the newly-built main road along which the nuclear missiles were due to be transported in a couple of days' time.

A little further off, Marc could just make out Fiveways: the big house in its own grounds in which Colette Russell lived with her parents. He made a mental note to pop by and say hello to her later.

'Morgan will see you now,' Radclyffe said. She spoke with an American accent and her face looked slightly familiar to Marc. He wondered where he had seen it before.

'Sure,' said Marc, and resisted a smile. The woman was acting as though Morgan was royalty, and that it was an honour to be admitted into her presence!

The door to the sitting-room opened and Morgan Knight walked in. Marc gulped. He'd seen her often enough around the school but she'd always remained aloof and unapproachable before. Now, with the January sun shining through the window and suffusing her long blonde hair with a golden glow, she looked absolutely stunning. Marc whistled silently to himself. Wouldn't some of the gang back at the

Institute be jealous of him now!

'Hi, you must be Marc,' she said, and indicated that he should sit down in one of the easy chairs by the window. She sat down in the one opposite him. Radclyffe said that she'd bring them some refreshments and left the room.

Morgan Knight was tall and statuesque with a porcelain-white complexion and deep and penetrating blue eyes. According to Liv Farrar, Morgan had been a rather mousy and gawky girl in spectacles when Liv had known her in the States. It seemed, thought Marc, as he reached into the pocket of his leather jacket for his list of questions, that, in the past year, the ugly duckling had definitely turned into a very sexy swan!

'Er, Liv said that you'd agreed to do this interview so that you wouldn't be bothered by everyone asking you questions about your dad,' Marc began.

'That's right,' Morgan said, and leant forward to look deeply into Marc's eyes. Marc found that he couldn't turn away from her. 'I don't understand all this interest in me and Dad,' she continued.

'Well, he has just gone halfway to Mars and back,' Marc said, as he looked down at his notes. *And his daughter is one of the sexiest things walking the face of the Earth!* he thought. *Those two good reasons are enough!*

'I suppose so,' Morgan said, with a modest smile.

'So what's it like up there?' Marc asked.

Morgan shut her eyes. 'Marvellous,' she breathed. 'So much space, so much emptiness. Knowing that you're the first person to be floating there in the space between the planets for millions and millions of years . . .'

'You sound as though you've been up there yourself,' Marc remarked.

Morgan opened her eyes. 'Of course not,' she said. 'That's just how Dad described it to me.'

'Yeah,' Marc said, as he remembered the TV news pictures of Armstrong Knight taking his walk on the outside of the *Deimos III*.

Those pictures had been pretty impressive. He and Rebecca had been glued to CNN for hours way back in March of last year, and not just because Rebecca's late father had once worked on the space program and had been there in the same mission control centre when the *Deimos I* had been launched.

The rest of the world seemed to have shared their view. After those live broadcasts, support for the space program had soared.

'Weren't you worried about your dad?' Marc asked. 'When those TV pictures went on the blink everyone thought something had gone majorly wrong.'

'Worried? Of course I wasn't worried,' Morgan lied. She frowned briefly, as though she was trying to recall a long-buried memory.

'So tell us more about your dad's spacewalk,' Marc urged her.

'It changed Dad so much,' Morgan remembered. 'We had a vacation in Sao Paulo–'

'Sao Paulo – in Brazil?' asked Marc.

'Yes,' Morgan replied. 'Why do you ask?'

'No reason,' Marc replied.

He knew that the Controller of the Project was based somewhere in that gigantic country, just as he knew his real identity. Marc had long since promised himself that Rebecca must never find out that the Project Controller was, in fact, her own father, who she believed to be dead. But it was surely just a coincidence that Morgan and her dad had visited that country. Of course they couldn't be involved in something as evil as the Project. He let Morgan continue.

'As I said, when he came back we went to Sao Paulo for a vacation and we talked about a lot of things then. He'd never been one for religion or thinking too much about philosophy and things like that before.'

'Yeah, I've heard that travelling in space can do that,' Marc said. 'Just looking down at the Earth from space kind of puts everything in perspective.'

'That's right,' Morgan said. 'When we were out there—'

'*We?*'

'Sorry, I mean, when my dad was out there, of course,' Morgan said, and seemed a little distressed at her slip of the tongue. 'When my dad was out there, he had – well, I suppose it was some sort of religious experience . . .'

Morgan stood up and walked over to the table by the window. A pile of leaflets was lying there and she picked one up and handed it over to Marc. It was the same poster that Rebecca and Joey had seen on the noticeboard of the Junior Common Room.

'The New Dawn?' Marc asked. 'What's that?'

'We believe that a great change is about to occur on the Earth,' Morgan said. 'We are small, but we are growing.'

Marc sighed. He'd heard all this millennium nonsense before and he couldn't bring himself to believe it. As far as he was concerned, such cults were dangerous. It would be a great pity if Morgan Knight and her dad had been taken in by all that kind of rubbish.

'The end of the world and all that?' he asked, trying to disguise his cynicism. 'Portents of doom and gloom if we all don't mend our ways?'

Morgan shook her head. 'Not the *end* of the world,' she said. 'The beginning of a new one.'

'I don't understand,' Marc admitted.

'The world is about to embark on a *new dawn* of peace and prosperity,' Morgan said. 'It is up to people like you and me to make sure that the world is ready for it.'

'You and me?' Marc was beginning not to like the sound of this.

'Of course,' Morgan said. 'You and me and everyone else at the Institute. Don't you see, Marc? We're different. Intelligent. Talented. Superior to the other ninety nine point nine per cent of the population. It's up to our kind to lead the weaker ones. Organise their lives, establish some order. Show them their right and proper place in this world. Make them realise who are the superior beings.'

'Hey, wait a minute,' Marc said. He definitely didn't like what he was hearing now. He was about to protest when the door opened and Radclyffe walked in. She was carrying a tray of sandwiches and two cans of decaffeinated Cola.

'What's wrong, Marc?' Morgan asked, and stared seductively at him with her deep blue eyes. She reached out for a cheese sandwich and offered the plate to Marc.

'Of course we're special,' Marc said, and took a ham sandwich. 'But so's everyone else. Every single person is special in their own way. No one's better than anyone just because they're brighter, or more talented, or attractive.'

'Do you *really* believe that, Marc?' she asked, never once taking her eyes off him.

'Yes,' Marc said. He chomped on his ham sandwich. Morgan's eyes were unnerving him now and he was beginning to feel a little awkward in her presence. 'If you automatically think that you're better than anyone else, then you're little more than a fascist. That's what the Nazis thought fifty years ago, and they slaughtered six million Jews to try and prove their point.'

Morgan smiled charitably. 'We're not fascists, Marc,' she assured him. 'We just want to help others, that's all. Show them the error of their ways. Cast out the unlike and prepare the planet for the New Dawn . . .'

Marc gulped down his sandwich and took the second one which Morgan offered him. 'No way do I believe that,' he said, and he felt a worry niggle at the back of his brain.

The way Morgan was talking reminded him of the

Project. From what he knew of them, it was clear that they believed they were above all laws; that they could do as they pleased with the ones they considered 'lesser' beings.

Marc knew that the Project was international, with its secret base hidden somewhere in South America. Morgan had mentioned a brief vacation there. Marc tried to banish his suspicions from his mind, gathered up his notes, and prepared to leave.

Morgan pouted sexily. 'Now, I've gone and upset you,' she said, and she sounded so disappointed that Marc was almost tempted to change his mind and stay.

'I'm sorry, Morgan,' he said, as she led him to the door. 'I'll never believe that anyone has a God-given right to rule other people like that.'

'If you came to the meeting I'm trying to organise at school?' she suggested. 'You'd meet some people at the Institute who think the way that I do. Maybe we can change your mind?'

Marc shook his head. 'Sorry,' he apologised once again.

'We can still be friends, can't we?' she asked.

'Of course,' Marc said. How could anyone not be friends with someone as attractive as Morgan Knight, no matter how dodgy her politics were?

'Then I'll see you soon,' Morgan said. She stood up and gave Marc a goodbye peck on the cheek.

As soon as the door closed on him Morgan turned to Radclyffe, who had remained in the room.

'He is ours,' Morgan said, and went over to the tray of snacks. She picked up a tomato sandwich.

'Of course,' Radclyffe said, and looked out of the window towards the Institute. 'And soon Axford's school will also be ours!'

Dateline: Fiveways;
Tuesday 12 January; 16.12.

'Count me out on this one, Colette!' Marc said, as Colette Russell handed him a leaflet advertising the planned demonstration against the nuclear missiles. He scanned the flyer and then folded it and put it into the back pocket of his jeans.

'Don't say you're siding with Eva?' Colette asked. Colette was a good-looking tomboy, whose shock of blonde hair and impish expression belied her wealthy and cultured upbringing.

'I thought you, of all people, didn't like Eva,' Griff said. When Marc had arrived at Fiveways, Griff had already been there. Marc suspected that Colette had invited him over because she had a crush on the good-natured and handsome eco-warrior.

'What d'you mean by that?' Marc asked, sharply.

Griff wondered what Marc was getting so upset about. 'Nothing special,' he said, truthfully. He reached out for one of the salmon sandwiches which Colette's father's housekeeper had left out for them. 'Everyone at the Institute has remarked how much you, Bec and Joey can't stand the Ice Queen.'

Marc shared a look with Colette and then turned

back to Griff. 'Well, maybe we know some things about Eva that you don't, Griff,' he said.

The Welsh boy with the long dreadlocked hair was interested now. 'Like what things?' he asked. There was a curious look in his eyes. It wasn't a look that particularly inspired confidence in Marc.

'Nothing we can prove, of course,' Colette began and then shut up. She realised that she had said too much.

'Nothing at all,' Marc lied.

Griff looked at Marc, and then at Colette, and then at Marc again. He shrugged. *Suit yourself*, his gesture seemed to say.

'So why aren't you going to help us stop the missiles being transported by the Institute?' he asked him once again.

'The sooner they're dumped and deactivated then the better,' Marc said. 'And besides, my grades have been slipping. If I don't put in more work then old Skinner is going to skin me alive.'

Griff smiled at the pun and at the mention of one of Marc's chemistry teachers. Ted Skinner was probably the most popular teacher at the Institute. Somewhere in his mid-sixties and unable to walk now without the aid of a stick, his liberal and generous attitude should have ensured that his pupils took advantage of him. On the contrary, his kindly and often bumbling manner only made them work harder for him. Everyone loved the old man, and that was probably a first for any teacher or lecturer at the Institute.

'He'll have to catch you first!' Griff joked.

'You must come and help us on the demo,' Colette urged Marc. 'Griff has been spending all of this week at school signing up people's names. He's been doing wonderful work.'

She gazed adoringly across at Griff and Marc smiled to himself. There was no doubt it: Colette had a definite crush on Griff! He'd better not mention it to the others, he decided; otherwise Joey would tease her mercilessly!

'Of course he has,' Marc agreed, but said that he was sorry, but he really did have to catch up with his studies. 'Besides, I said I'd help out Johnny Lau with some of his work.'

'Yes, Rebecca mentioned that on the phone,' Colette told him. She looked thoughtfully at Marc. 'Do you like Johnny, Marc?'

'He seems a nice enough bloke,' Marc admitted, and Colette recalled how Rebecca had also told her that Marc had been particularly abrupt with Johnny earlier. 'Yes, I do like him. Don't you?'

'I've only met him once,' she reminded him. 'I just got the idea that he's hiding something, that's all.'

'Yes, Joey told me,' Marc remembered.

'He's seems OK to me,' Griff joined in. 'He said that he supported what I was doing.'

'He's going to join the protest too?' asked Colette.

'No,' came back the reply. 'He wouldn't give me a reason, either.'

'He's an Oriental,' Marc said. 'I always thought his kind–'

'*His kind*?' asked Colette. The words sounded a little

suspect, even vaguely racist. In fact, coming from Marc's lips, they sounded distinctly odd.

'Sorry,' Marc said. He realised how his words could have been misinterpreted. He corrected himself. 'I always thought people from his culture were pacifists.'

'So am I,' Griff said. 'But that doesn't mean you can't make a non-violent protest against the missiles.'

'Sorry, Griff, but I can't join you and Colette,' he repeated.

'Traitor,' said Colette lightly, and smiled.

'Even if I didn't have Skinner's work to catch up on, I've still got to write up my article for *The Enquirer*.'

'You working for Liv Farrar?' Griff asked.

'That's right,' Marc said, and then shared a grin with Griff. 'I've just been interviewing Morgan Knight. She might have some dodgy political ideas, Griff, but take it from me, she is *hot*!'

'Who's Morgan Knight?' asked Colette uncertainly, not at all liking the direction this conversation was taking.

'Armstrong Knight's daughter, and the sexiest thing in the world,' Marc told her. 'Every guy's crazy about her!'

'I'm sure Griff isn't,' Colette said, and smiled, looking for reassurance from the Welsh boy.

Griff returned the smile, but then a change seemed to come over him. The smile turned into a scowl. He swung his head around to look at Marc.

'So you fancy Morgan Knight, do you?' he asked.

'Doesn't everyone?'

Griff raised a pierced eyebrow in disdain and

sneered. 'And someone like you seriously thinks that he has a chance with her?'

Marc looked slightly put out and glanced at his reflection in the living-room mirror. He was no Leonardo DiCaprio or Brad Pitt, but he reckoned he wasn't too bad.

'Well, yes,' he said. 'As good a chance as anyone else.'

'Who do you think you're kidding?' Griff said. The expression on his face was even darker now.

'Griff, stop it,' Colette said. She was feeling distinctly uncomfortable and she could sense danger in the room.

'You're just a jumped-up kid on a scholarship who thinks he's God's gift to women,' Griff continued. 'So leave her alone, you hear? Girls like Morgan aren't for the likes of you–'

'Hey, now wait a minute!' Marc stood up and pointed a warning finger at Griff. Griff sprang to his feet and stared wildly at Marc.

'You threatening me?'

'Of course Marc isn't threatening you,' Colette said, in an attempt to defuse the potentially nasty situation.

Marc ignored Colette and returned Griff's challenging stare. 'Yeah,' he said. 'As a matter of fact I *am* threatening you!'

Griff snarled and pushed Marc. Marc fell backwards on to the floor and Griff leapt on top of him.

The Welsh boy spat at Marc like a wild animal and raised a fist to punch Marc in the face. Marc moved his head away just in time and Griff's hand smashed into the carpet. He yowled with pain.

Marc took advantage of this momentary diversion and managed to push Griff off him. He leapt up to move away, but Griff was too quick for him. Griff darted out his leg and tripped him up. Marc crashed down to the floor once more, knocking over a small table and a glass vase, which smashed to the ground into a hundred pieces.

Marc rolled over on to his back to see Griff bear down on him. He lashed out with his hands and managed to deal Griff a glancing blow on the chin. Blood started to trickle from the corners of Griff's mouth.

The taste of his own blood enraged Griff even more. He reached out for one of the shards of broken glass on the carpet and aimed for Marc's throat.

'Stop it!' Colette cried. She tried to pull Griff off Marc, but succeeded only in knocking the sliver of glass out of his hand. 'Stop it before you kill each other!'

'His kind shouldn't be allowed to live!' Griff growled. He rammed a fist into Marc's face.

'I'll see you dead, you Welsh scumbag!' Marc said. He reached out for Griff's dreadlocks and yanked hard. Tears appeared in Griff's eyes.

'Stop it!' Colette screamed again. She pulled at Griff once more; it was useless – he was far too strong for her. In his maddened state, he was probably far too strong for anyone, she realised.

'Marc! Griff! You're behaving like animals!' she cried out, and scrunched her eyes tightly, as if to cut out the vision of two of her friends beating each other to within an inch of their lives.

Colette concentrated, willing Marc and Griff to stop fighting, not quite knowing what she was doing, but hoping that the psychic powers that she shared with Joey could, in some way, calm down the two blood-hungry boys. *Peace. Calm. Contentment. Out with the evil. In with the good. No more fighting. No more hate. No more . . .*

Everything fell silent and Colette opened her eyes. Her calming thoughts, amplified by her psychic talents, had worked their desired effect.

Marc and Griff were sitting on the carpet, facing each other, with blood now streaming from both their mouths. No longer was there a look of hatred on each of their faces. Now there was only an expression of disbelief, mixed with horror, and blank incomprehension.

Griff was the first to speak. 'I . . . I don't know what came over me . . .' he said weakly, and shook his head.

'You were . . . you were going to kill me . . .' Marc said, and then realised with a terrible clarity: 'I was going to kill you too . . .'

'Why?' Colette asked, as she helped them both to their feet. Marc stared strangely at Griff.

'He's different . . . foreign' he finally said.

'Don't be stupid,' Colette said, 'he's only Welsh.'

'No, he was . . . *unlike*,' Marc said slowly, as Morgan Knight's strange phrase resounded eerily in his mind.

Cast out the unlike . . . cast out the unlike . . . cast out . . .

'And I hated you too,' Griff realised. 'You reminded

me of all those English who come to Wales, buying their holiday cottages and forcing people off the land they've been living on for centuries. My dad has never liked the English. He says it was the English Parliament who closed down the mines all those years ago.'

Marc harrumphed awkwardly. 'Look, let's forget about it, shall we?' he said, and extended his hand. 'I'm sorry. Mates again?'

Griff smiled just as awkwardly and took Marc's hand. 'I'm sorry too,' he said genuinely. 'Mates again.'

'Good!' said Colette, and smiled gratefully. The smile was for the boys' sake. In her heart Colette was terrified.

She had sensed and witnessed pure and unchecked hatred in the room. Griff, the pacifist, and Marc, who only ever raised a hand in self-defence, had nearly killed each other.

For a minute, they had given in to their baser and most evil instincts. For a minute, Marc and Griff had reverted to being savages.

And, somehow, Morgan Knight was behind it all.

Dateline: Study Bedroom A313, The Institute; Tuesday 12 January; 19.11.

'This is really sweet of you, Joey,' Rebecca said, as the lift doors opened on the third floor of the boys' hostel in the Institute grounds.

Joey winced. In his fourteen years he'd been insulted by the best, but if there was one thing in the world Joey Williams hated being described as, it was 'sweet'.

'Hey, leave it out,' he said. He started to make his way down the corridor to Room A313. 'I want to apologise to Johnny. I was a real dork to him earlier today. Maybe I can help him out with his biology assignment to make up for it.'

'Everyone's been a real dork today,' Rebecca said. 'Marc included.'

'Where's he now?' Joey wanted to know.

Rebecca shrugged. She had no idea, she told Joey. Before coming to visit him, she'd knocked on Marc's door. There had been no reply and the guy next door had told her that he hadn't seen him all day. If he knew Marc, he'd told her with a knowing twinkle in his eyes, he'd be over at the girls' hostel, helping out with a party that Christina Haack was organising. The popular and friendly physics student from Berlin had just gained a string of three As for her holiday assignments and, as far as she was concerned, that was excuse enough for a party. Her dad had agreed with her and given her a large wodge of cash with which to celebrate. Even though she was in the Upper Sixth, Christina's parties were open to everyone aged fourteen and over.

'No matter what your opinion is, I still think what you're doing is real sweet,' Rebecca said.

'Thank you – *not*,' mumbled Joey. 'So why did you want to come?'

'Like you, I thought I'd help Johnny out too,' she

said. 'To make up for Marc being such a louse to him this afternoon.'

'And the other reason?' asked Joey, who didn't need any psychic powers to know when Rebecca wasn't telling the entire truth.

'Eva told us not to mix with Johnny again,' she replied. 'And that's reason enough. I want to find out why she's so anxious for us not to see him.'

'She said that our scholarships would be in danger if we disobeyed her.'

'Then we'd better make sure that she doesn't find out, hadn't we?'

Rebecca looked out through the corridor window at the dark and brooding shape of the main Institute building with its dark mock-Gothic colonnades, tall shuttered windows and its turrets, which Joey had once described as belonging more to an episode of *The Addams Family* than to a high-flying science school. Lights were still burning in many of the laboratory windows there.

A little way off and connected to the main building by a covered walkway was the admin block. That old ramshackle building was, some said, all that remained of the old manor house which had stood on the site for hundreds of years, after the old abbey had been torn down.

All but two windows there were dark: the ones belonging to the office of General Axford and Eva. It seemed that they were safe from Eva's all-prying eyes for the moment, at least.

'She wouldn't carry out her threat, anyway,' Joey

said confidently as they approached the door to Room A313.

'How do you come to that brilliant conclusion?' Rebecca said. 'You going in for a spot of fortune-telling now, as well as all your other psychic powers?'

Joey grinned. 'No such luck,' he said. 'We know too much about Eva now and her connection to the Project. She wouldn't dare kick us out of the Institute.'

'We have no certain proof,' Rebecca pointed out. 'All we know is that she's *probably* connected with the Project in some way.'

'Me and Marc recognised her back in the sewers,' Joey reminded her, referring to the time when they'd visited London and had come across the horrors of the Alien Circus in the capital's East End. 'She might be Axford's assistant but she's also the Deputy Controller of the Project.'

'Maybe,' Rebecca said, careful not to commit herself. Her own memories of that time were particularly hazy, the result of her having been infected by some weird kind of alien virus. 'You never clearly saw her, you told me. She always kept to the shadows. All you found in the end was a broken pair of dark glasses which could have belonged to anyone.'

'That's proof enough for me.'

'But not for me,' said Rebecca. 'And as for her being Deputy Controller of the Project ... heck, we don't know what the Project really is.'

'The bad guys, that's what!' Joey quipped grimly,

and then rapped smartly on the door to Johnny Lau's study bedroom.

'Enter.' Johnny's curiously formal voice came from within the room. Joey opened the door and walked in, followed by Rebecca.

Study bedroom A313 was larger than most, so large in fact that there was room for an ornate oriental-style room divider, which effectively divided the room in half.

Johnny was sitting at his desk watching Channel Four News on a small portable TV. The reporter was winding up a boring report on some border disputes in the Far East between China and the small independent state of Zhou-zhun.

Zhou-zhun had been a part of China until quite recently, when it had gained its independence from its begrudging former masters together with some valuable mineral deposits on its soil, as well as some military hardware. Johnny hastily clicked off the TV and turned around to greet his guests.

While Joey made his apologies for his gross attitude earlier that day, Rebecca took time to look around Johnny's room. Apart from its size and its unusual tidiness, it was pretty much like any other study bedroom at the Institute.

Johnny's shelves creaked under the weight of scores of heavy textbooks. There were volumes on physics and chemistry and biology, of course, as well as books on other aspects of the National Curriculum, which – even as specialised science students – every pupil at the Institute had to follow.

The books appeared to be brand-new and looked as though they'd hardly ever been opened. She remembered Joey telling her about Johnny's bad grades. *Well he'd better start taking his books down from the shelves more often if he doesn't want to lose his place here*, she thought.

While Joey leafed through the papers in Johnny's biology file, Rebecca walked over to the bookshelves. She loved inspecting other people's reading material and knew that the volumes someone chooses to put on their bookshelves often reveal a lot about the person.

Johnny's books did no such thing, largely because many of the titles were in what she thought was Chinese. One book took her eye, however: a large, thin volume bound in red leather with gilt edging. She took it down and examined the elaborate dragon-crest on the book's cover.

'You mustn't.'

Johnny stood up, crossed over and took the book from Rebecca. He didn't put it back on the shelf, but instead placed it in the top left-hand drawer of his desk and locked it with a key.

'Sorry,' Rebecca said, and rejoined Johnny and Joey by the desk. 'I didn't mean to pry.'

'Do not worry,' Johnny said. 'No offence was taken.' He turned back to the papers on his desk. 'I appreciate the fact that you are helping me with my assignment.'

'It's the least we can do,' Rebecca said, and pulled up a chair. 'So what's the big problem?'

She and Joey peered at the test questions which Axford had set Johnny for the Christmas vacation.

Beneath the questions, Johnny had scribbled some notes to help him answer the questions correctly. Rebecca frowned. With some answers Johnny was on the right lines; with others he was wildly wrong.

She jabbed a finger at one question, which centred around the various functions of the brain. Johnny had scribbled a large red question mark there.

'Serotonin.' She read out the word which he had ringed in red.

'Yes,' Johnny said, and looked eagerly at Rebecca for an answer. 'What is it? I have looked in my books but I cannot find any reference to it.'

'It's a neurotransmitter,' she said, knowledgeably. Johnny was none the wiser.

'I'm sorry?' he asked. 'It is what? I do not understand the word.'

Rebecca looked a little suspiciously at Johnny. She wouldn't have expected a normal fourteen-year-old to know what a neurotransmitter was. But Johnny Lau wasn't a normal student, she reminded herself, Johnny Lau was an Institute student.

Or was he?

Colette and Joey had both thought that he was a fraud. And what was it that Eva had told them? *Neither of you will associate with Lau Teng Lee again*, she had said. What was it that she was afraid they might find out?

'It's a chemical which transmits messages from one brain cell to another,' she explained. By her side, Joey had got bored. He stood up and walked over to the large dividing screen.

'Of course it is,' Johnny said. 'I had forgotten.'

I bet . . . Joey thought. He started to pull back the screen.

'Serotonin is responsible for mood swings,' Rebecca told Johnny. 'When there's just enough serotonin swimming around in your brain, then you're happy and contented.'

'And when there's too little?'

'Freak-Out City,' Rebecca said. 'You get moody and depressed; violent even. The brain's a real weird thing, Johnny. It's dangerous to mess around with it.'

'Thank you,' Johnny said, and started to note down what Rebecca had told him when an appreciative whistle from Joey stopped him.

'Will you take a look at this!' he cried out. 'Man, but this sure is some serious hardware.'

'No, you mustn't!' Johnny said. 'No! Don't!' He rushed over to where Joey had pulled back the screen to reveal a bank of impressive-looking equipment.

It was too late. Joey was already inspecting the gear, with the same excitement he'd experienced when he come across Sony Playstations for the first time.

'You mustn't tell anyone about this!' Johnny said, as Rebecca came over to join them.

She looked at the bank of monitor screens linked up to what appeared to be computer keyboards and hard disks, but which, she suspected, served another purpose. They reminded her a little of a mini-version of the bank of monitors she had been watching on CNN with Marc during Armstrong Knight's spacewalk last year.

Joey looked suspiciously at Johnny. Something had really upset the guy, he knew. He wondered what it was. He looked deep into the Chinese boy's eyes, trying to get a hint of what was troubling him.

Nothing.

'What's all that equipment for?' Rebecca asked, as Johnny hastily replaced the oriental screen.

Johnny had no time to answer. There was a crashing sound and the window to Johnny's room smashed as something was thrown through it.

Then something else was thrown in through the open window, something which exploded with a *whumph!* on the carpeted floor. The whole place started to go up in flames. Tongues of fire licked at the curtains.

'Get out!' Joey said. He pushed Johnny and Rebecca towards the door. All three of them stumbled out into the corridor. Joey grabbed the small fire extinguisher on the landing and went back into the room.

The fire hadn't yet caught effective hold and it was a relatively simple matter for Joey to douse the flames. As soon as the fire had been put out, he and Rebecca looked at Johnny. His face was as white as a sheet.

'They have found me,' he muttered to himself.

'Found you?' asked Joey. 'Who have found you, Johnny?'

'Please do not ask me that,' said Johnny.

Rebecca went over and picked up the brick which had first been thrown through the window. A sheet of paper had been wrapped around it, which she unfurled.

It was a flyer advertising Griff's forthcoming demonstration against the nuclear missiles, but it wasn't that which interested Rebecca. She turned it over and read the note which had been scrawled on the other side.

KEEP THE INSTITUTE PURE
CAST OUT THE UNLIKE!

'Sick,' she said, and went over to the open window and peered out. Someone was running away from the boys' hostel and back in the direction of the main Institute building.

It was dark and the culprit was already some distance away – Rebecca didn't mention it to Joey or to Johnny.

For she couldn't be sure, but the person who had thrown the brick in through the window looked a lot like Marc.

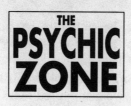

THE PSYCHIC ZONE

3

Recruitment

Dateline: General Axford's Office, The Institute;
Wednesday 13 January; 08.47.

Joey shuffled uneasily in the long uncomfortable sofa. That was only to be expected. Every other time he had sat on this sofa it had been while waiting for a reprimand for a piece of homework handed in late, or a lecture that he had missed because he'd been too busy surfing the Net. This, however, was the first time he'd come here voluntarily and he was already considering it to be a pretty bad move.

He looked up gloomily at the sign on the door by which he was sitting.

General A.C. Axford, OBE, M.Phil, B.Sc
Principal

That was what the sign read. As far as Joey was concerned, what it spelt was trouble – and trouble with a capital 'T', at that.

There was a large potted palm and a small fish tank on a table. They were supposed to be there to instil a sense of calm in anyone who was waiting for an audience with General Axford.

They weren't working. To Joey, the potted palm was about as calming as a Triffid and the tank might as well have been filled with piranhas for all the reassurance it was giving him. He looked at Rebecca, who was sitting beside him.

'Are you sure that this is such a good idea?' he asked her. Rebecca looked shocked.

'Of course it's a good idea!' she said.

'But Johnny said that he didn't want to make a fuss,' Joey said, recalling the conversation they had had with Johnny after the brick had been thrown through his window.

'Then he's crazy,' Rebecca said. 'Someone threw a brick *and* a firebomb into Johnny's window last night. It was a blatantly racist attack. General Axford must be told about it.'

'Yeah, sure,' Joey said, not sounding sure at all. 'But maybe it was a one-off. And it's not as if he wasn't asking for it.'

This Rebecca couldn't believe. 'What are you saying?' she asked.

'Well, it's not like he makes an effort to mix with anyone else,' Joey said, and wondered why his head suddenly seemed to be hurting so much. These headaches – or was it really just the same headache? – were getting worse and worse. It looked as though he were about to come down with a major migraine. 'All he does is hang about in his room. He never joins in anything or goes to any parties – at least not as far as I know. I know that Christina's invited him to her party tonight and I bet that he won't come. If people are pushing him around then he's only got himself to blame.'

'Like you only had yourself to blame when the white kids back in New York called you a filthy nigger?' Rebecca reminded him.

Joey frowned and shook his head. He realised what he'd just said. 'I'm sorry,' he said. 'I don't know what came over me. Of course Johnny didn't bring it on himself.'

'Of course he didn't,' Rebecca agreed, She smoothed out the piece of paper which had been wrapped around the brick.

KEEP THE INSTITUTE PURE!
CAST OUT THE UNLIKE!

The written words sent a shiver down her spine.

'You know what this reminds me of?' she asked.

'No,' said Joey. 'What?'

'Something my old grandma – Dad's mom – told me happened when she was a teenager,' Rebecca said. 'She lived in Germany and won a place to study physics at the Humboldt University in Berlin.'

'Brains run in the family then,' Joey said, with a smile.

'But she wasn't allowed to go there,' Rebecca continued. 'She was Jewish, you see, and when the Nazis came to power that meant she was scum and not fit to live. But she was lucky. Boy, was she lucky. Her folks had money and the family emigrated to the States. They got out just in time. Shortly after that, the Nazis started sending the Jews off to the gas chambers.'

'Bastards,' Joey said. 'I remember an article that Liv wrote in *The Enquirer* a couple of months back. It sure made my blood run cold.'

'The Nazis wanted to keep, first Germany, and then the entire world, "pure". They wanted to get rid of all the Jews and the blacks and the gays and anyone else who didn't agree with them, or fit in with their perverted idea of a "perfect" world.'

Rebecca looked down at the piece of paper in her hand. 'They wanted to "cast out the unlike",' she said. 'And that's why I think that General Axford should be told of the attack on Johnny last night. It was clearly racist.'

'But who could have done it?' asked Joey.

'I don't know,' Rebecca lied.

She remembered the figure she had seen running away from the boys' hostel. Had it *really* been Marc? Had it really been the guy who was her best friend and who had gone with her last year to that Anti-Racism demonstration in London's Trafalgar Square?

She had rung Christina Haack last night, who had told her that Marc hadn't been helping her with the preparations for tonight's party as they had assumed.

So just where had he been when someone had firebombed Johnny Lau's room?

'You seen Marc today?' she asked Joey, trying to make the question seem as casual as possible.

Joey shook his head. 'I called round after we left Johnny's room,' he said. 'Seems like he wasn't with Christina after all. I guess he was still in the village at Morgan's – lucky so-and-so.'

'Of course,' said Rebecca.

'You jealous?'

'Grow up!'

'He'd've been really interested in that hardware in Johnny's room,' Joey said. 'You know what it was?'

Rebecca remembered the banks of screens in Johnny's room which had reminded her of similar ones at Mission Control in Houston. Even though Rebecca didn't live on-site at the Institute she knew that every study bedroom there was equipped with a PC and access to the World Wide Web. The hardware in Johnny's room, however, was pretty spectacular – especially for a guy who clearly wasn't the most scientifically-gifted person in the world.

'You tell me,' she said to Joey.

'Monitoring and communications equipment,' he told her. 'Half of it with satellite links, I bet. I reckon that Johnny could contact anywhere in the world within seconds. Who knows? Maybe out in space, as well.'

'But what would he need it for?' Rebecca wondered.

However, before Joey could answer her question,

the door to General Axford's office opened. Eva peered down at them through her dark glasses.

'The General will see you now,' she informed them coldly. (In fact, General Axford had been ready to see Rebecca and Joey for the past five minutes. It was just that Eva liked to keep people waiting.)

Rebecca and Joey followed Eva into the office where General Axford was waiting for them. Eva showed them to the two chairs in front of the Principal's desk and then resumed her place at her own desk at the far end of the room. She started to sort through some papers, but Rebecca and Joey both knew that she'd be listening to – and remembering – every word they'd be saying.

'Please sit down, Miss Storm, Mr Williams,' General Axford said, in his usual clipped and militarily-precise voice. Despite the fact that he was confined to an electric wheelchair, the gaunt and grey-haired fifty-something Principal of the Institute was still an imposing and impressive man, whose piercing-blue eyes could make even the most self-assured student tremble with apprehension.

Rebecca and Joey did as they were told. General Axford sat back in his wheelchair and regarded them across his desk.

'So, Miss Storm, you have requested an interview with me,' he said, and smiled. 'That is very gratifying, if unusual. It's normally myself, or Eva, who ask to see certain students.'

Axford's pleasant manner didn't fool either of them for an instant. Nevertheless, Rebecca told him what had happened last night.

One of the Institute's foreign students had been attacked, she told him. A firebomb had been thrown in through their window. There was no telling who they might target next. She took the piece of paper with the racist taunt and slammed it down in front of General Axford.

General Axford seemed to be unimpressed, as he read the paper and then turned it over to see the advertisement for the demonstration against the nuclear missiles. He smiled his false smile once again.

'There are no racists here at the Institute, Miss Storm,' he reassured her. 'Eva and myself wouldn't allow it. If there were, then they would be expelled immediately.'

'You tell that to Johnny then,' Joey said.

'Johnny?' Axford's smile faded.

'Yeah, Johnny Lau,' Joey said. 'He was the guy those scumbags targeted last night.'

'You were expressly forbidden ever to associate with Lau Teng Lee again,' Eva said, from her desk (from where she wasn't supposed to be listening). Rebecca returned Eva's icy remark with an even icier stare.

'If we'd've done what you'd told us, then Johnny might be dead by now,' she said. 'It was Joey who put out the fire in his room.'

Eva was about to say something else, but Axford interrupted her – a first in itself.

'The attack was made on Lau Teng Lee?' he asked. There was an urgent and worried look in his eyes.

'On Johnny Lau, yes,' Rebecca confirmed, and was surprised at the reaction she caused in both Axford and Eva. Axford's face fell into a mask of frightened despair and there was even a nervous twitch at the side of Eva's mouth.

'No harm must come to Lau Teng Lee,' Axford said to Eva, no longer seeming even to know that Rebecca and Joey were in the room.

'He must be protected,' Eva agreed, and started to scribble down some notes on the jotter on her desk. 'For his own good, of course.'

'What are you suggesting?' Rebecca asked them. General Axford looked up from his desk at her.

'You may go now, children,' he said.

'You haven't answered Rebecca's question,' Joey pointed out angrily.

General Axford considered Joey with a hard glare. It didn't phase out Joey.

'As Miss Storm has pointed out, there is indeed a racist element at our Institute,' Axford said, and was about to say more when Rebecca interrupted him.

'That's not what you said a couple of minutes ago,' Rebecca reminded him. 'You said that such things were unthinkable at the Institute.'

'Then let us think the unthinkable,' Axford said. 'If there is a racist element at the Institute then it must be stamped out.'

'Yeah, well, that's what I think too,' Rebecca said, a little uneasily. There was a strange violence to the General's words. 'But why now? There are kids from every corner of the world here at the Institute: black, brown, white, red, yellow. Nothing like this has ever happened before.'

'The Institute must be kept pure,' Eva intoned, reminding Rebecca and Joey of the words on the racist paper thrown into Johnny's window. 'And it must be seen to be kept pure also. Dissent must not be allowed to thrive. It must be burnt out.'

'And Lau Teng Lee must come to no harm,' General Axford said. He read once again the reverse side of the racist message of hate and then aimed his eyes at Rebecca and Joey once again. 'And this demonstration against the nuclear missiles must not be allowed to go ahead. Is that understood?'

'You'd better ask Griff about that,' Rebecca said. 'He's the guy who's organising it. We're not responsible for anything he does.'

'Then I am holding you responsible, Miss Storm,' Axford said. 'Persuade this–' He looked not at Rebecca or Joey, but at his personal assistant. 'What is the boy's name again, Eva?'

'Griff Rhys-Jenkins,' she said, without consulting any source of information apart from her own encyclopaedic knowledge of everything and everyone at the Institute. 'Brilliant physics student but with some suspect political inclinations. Pacifism, for instance. He's a young member of CND, Friends of the Earth, and several other subversive groups.' Then she added, not quite under her breath; 'Not really *our* sort.'

'And we allow him to study here?' Axford asked, once again ignoring Rebecca and Joey's presence in the office.

'His father has made substantial donations to the school, General,' Eva informed him.

'Of course,' General Axford said, and Rebecca and Joey both knew what that meant. General Axford was prepared to ignore any manner of indiscretions as long as money was coming in to the Institute. For him, the continued future well-being of his precious Institute was the only thing which really mattered to him.

And it was that knowledge which prompted Joey to ask his next question. 'I'd've thought that you and Eva would be the first ones to support Griff's protest,' he said.

'And how do you come to that conclusion, Mr Williams?' he asked.

'Well, like, these missiles are gonna get real near to the Institute, aren't they?' he said. 'So what happens if something goes wrong? What happens if they go off? Bang! No more missiles. No more Institute, for that matter.'

'Not to mention the fall-out. It could leave the countryside around here off-limits for years, centuries even,' Rebecca said.

She remembered one of General Axford's rare lectures to the Institute students. He had talked about his service in the Gulf War. Even though that conflict hadn't been nuclear, it had still left its own trail of devastation. There had even been talk of biological warfare. Axford had condemned all that destruction. It was unusual for him to support the (admittedly) slim possibility of such a nightmare now visiting the Institute.

For a second Rebecca and Joey thought that they had got through to Axford. There was an uncertain look on his face and, as in all such instances, he turned to Eva for advice.

Eva nodded almost imperceptibly to the General. Joey didn't miss it and, not for the first time, wondered just what sort of hold Eva had over Axford.

The General turned back to Rebecca and Joey. 'The missiles pose no danger to the Institute,' he said finally. 'And the demonstration will *not* take place, Miss Storm.'

'But–' Rebecca started to protest.

'You *will* see to it, won't you, Miss Storm?' said Eva. It was phrased as a request but Rebecca knew that it was a command.

'Look, Griff's organising the action, not me,' Rebecca protested. 'Why don't you ask him?'

Eva opened her drawer and pulled out a red cardboard folder, which she took over to Axford and then she returned to her desk. Axford took out the computer print-out contained in the folder, checked up on some figures, and then smiled at Rebecca once again – with all the friendliness of a king cobra ready to strike.

'I see your fees for this term are not yet paid in full, Miss Storm,' he said, almost casually.

Rebecca blushed, embarrassed. It was true. Part of her fees were paid by a scholarship grant, but the remainder were billed to her scientist mother, Emma.

'Ah, well, er, Mom says they'll be in any day now,'

she blustered. 'One of her jobs for the Ministry fell through at the last minute. Things have been kinda tight moneywise.'

Rebecca glared at Eva. There should have been no reason for the Ministry of Technocratic Planning and Development suddenly and inexplicably pulling the plug on one of Emma Storm's research projects. It wasn't as if the Government was strapped for cash these days.

Rebecca had suspected Eva's involvement. But, just as she couldn't prove Eva's links with the Project, so she couldn't find any concrete evidence for her interference in her mother's work. Eva was far too clever for that. Eva was far too clever for anyone.

'Be that as it may,' General Axford continued, 'the Institute rules clearly state that a student's complete fees must be paid *in full* on the first day of each term. Otherwise ... well, I don't have to tell you the consequences, do I, Miss Storm?'

'No, sir,' Rebecca said, and lowered her eyes. 'I'll see what I can do.'

'Just ensure that the demonstration doesn't go ahead,' Axford said with a final smile. 'Now you may both go.'

Rebecca and Joey left the room, but not before noticing Eva quit her desk again and engage in an animated discussion with the General. They wondered what the two were talking about. They were both clearly agitated and worried.

Joey let out a whistle as soon as the door had closed behind him. 'Well, what about that?' he said.

'I don't understand it,' Rebecca said. 'As soon as we mentioned that Johnny was the subject of the racist attack, Axford completely changed his tune. Why?'

'Like I said, you can't trust the . . .' Joey didn't allow himself to finish the sentence.

Instead, he shook his head and tried to ease away with his fingers the headache which he could still feel building up inside him. 'Like I said, there's something which isn't quite right about Johnny.'

'And you still don't know what it is?' she asked.

'No,' said Joey. 'Last night, just before the attack, I tried to "zap" Johnny.'

'I thought you didn't like peeking into other people's minds like that,' Rebecca said, as they headed out of the old admin building along the covered walkway and to the main Institute block.

'I don't,' he said. 'But after Colette had said that she didn't trust the guy, and when I saw all that hi-tech equipment in his room, I got to wondering who he really was.'

'And?' asked Rebecca. 'What did you see?'

'Nothing,' Joey said. 'Zilch. One big fat zero.' He rammed his hands into his pockets as they walked through the double doors of the main building and made their way to the Junior Common Room. 'Maybe I was just having a bad day,' he said, trying to sound nonchalant. 'Anyway, what are you going to do about the demonstration?'

'I can't ask Griff to stop it,' Rebecca said, as they approached the noticeboard. 'But if I don't, then I might lose my place at the Institute. I can't face that either.'

'You're up the creek without a paddle, huh?' Joey asked, sympathetically.

'You're telling me,' Rebecca said, gloomily. She paused to look at the notices pinned up on the board.

Stop the Carriers of Death! Protect the Institute! Do you really want Brentmouth village to become another Hiroshima? Do you really want to be fried? one proclaimed. She smiled in spite of herself. It seemed that Griff had decided that his serious but mildly-worded flyers for the demo weren't doing the trick and he'd decided to take a more lurid approach.

'I can't understand why Axford and Eva are so keen on stopping the demonstration,' Joey said.

'It won't be the first time,' Rebecca recalled. 'Eva likes order and discipline at the Institute. The Christian society, the Judaic Studies society and the other religious groups she allows to carry on – probably because she regards religion as nothing more than superstition. But anything else which poses a threat to the well-ordered running of things ... Only last term she ordered our local branch of Amnesty to disband. Said that the interests of political prisoners overseas were not the proper interests of an Institute student.'

'She was probably scared that we'd find out about some of the Project's more shady goings-on,' Joey said. He shut up as he saw a tall blonde-haired girl walk along the corridor, carrying a rolled-up poster.

'Hi, Christina,' Rebecca said, recognising the grade-A physics student.

'*Guten tag,*' Christina said, and gave them both a welcoming peck on the cheek.

Joey looked down at the poster in Christina's hand. 'You still advertising for your gig tonight?' he asked. 'I thought that the whole Institute knew about it, the way you've been talking!'

Christina giggled. 'Everyone who is anyone will be at my party tonight!' she announced proudly. 'General Axford has allowed me to use the main Assembly Hall.'

'That must have taken some doing,' Rebecca said, but Christina shook her head.

'My father offered to make a donation to the new science block, if I could have my party at the Institute, rather than in the village. He is worried that some of the village boys might try and crash the party. You know what those kind of boys are like.'

'See, Rebecca?' Joey said. 'It all comes down to money in the end.'

'Don't I know it!' she said, and reminded herself to have a quiet word with her mother about her school fees when she got home that night.

'You are both coming, *ja*?' Christina asked. 'And your friend, Colette, from the village, of course.'

'I thought the party was just for Institute students?' Rebecca asked.

'But Colette is your friend, Rebecca, and you know that any friend of yours is a friend of mine also!'

'Thanks, Christina, you're a real pal,' Rebecca said, and pointed to the rolled-up poster once again. 'So what's the poster about?'

'Just something I said I would put up for a friend,' Christina said. However, before she could say more,

69

Joey clutched his stomach and groaned.

'C'mon, Rebecca!' he said. 'I'm starved. I haven't had any breakfast yet, y'know!'

'OK,' Rebecca said, and checked her watch. 'We've still got some time to go before our first class. Tell you what, I'll stand you a bowl of muesli and an orange juice.'

'I'd much rather have one of those real big English fry-ups with chips.'

'Yuk,' said Rebecca, but agreed that she'd have the muesli and he could have the sausage, bacon and fries.

After they had gone, Christina unrolled the poster and pinned it carefully on the noticeboard. The poster was so large that it partly covered two other notices: one reminding Institute students that all fees were to be paid promptly and another extolling the delights of a break (cost £500 per person for the week) at the Institute's study centre up near Castlecraig in north-east Scotland. However, Christina took great care not to cover any part of Griff's poster for the forthcoming demo.

She stood back and looked at her work. She smiled. Morgan would be so proud of her, she thought. At the moment, pleasing Morgan Knight was the most important thing in Christina's life.

After tonight's party, that was.

The New Dawn for a New Millennium

Stand Apart From The Unlike
Meet Today and Realise Your True Worth!

*Wednesday 13 January; 16.00; Junior Common Room;
Refreshments Provided*

*Dateline: Junior Common Room, The Institute;
Wednesday 13 January; 16.11.*

The Junior Common Room was only half-full when
the meeting of the New Dawn began. Morgan Knight
wasn't that worried though, as she looked from the
centre of the room at the chairs which had been set
around her in a circle.

Some of the brightest brains at the Institute had
come to the meeting, although whether it was out of
genuine interest or because of the opportunity to skive
off the last period of the day and get some free food,
she couldn't be certain.

Their reasons did not overly concern Morgan. These
people were the cream of the Institute's crop, the ones
who were destined in a few years' time to become
top-flyers in the worlds of science and technocracy
and government. They were the students who had
gained almost universal respect from their fellow
Institute students. They were the people that *mattered*.

There was the sandy-haired and conventionally
good-looking Calvin Charles, whose run of almost
straight As in his chemistry exams was almost as good
as Christina Haack's. She was sitting beside him,
before going on to her party later. There was Marc
Price, of course, who was looking at her with clearly-

smitten eyes. Griff Rhys-Jenkins too, who was so concerned that his precious little missiles wouldn't go anywhere near the Institute.

Morgan failed to spot Joey in the crowd, or Liv Farrar, the editor of *The Enquirer*, but she did see Rebecca. She was standing at the back of the room, by the door. There was a concerned expression on her face as Morgan told of how her father had first discovered the secrets of the New Dawn after he had returned from his mission to Mars. Next to Rebecca was a girl who Morgan didn't recognise, and Marc told her that it was his friend, Colette. He'd introduce her to Morgan later, if she wanted. Morgan said no. Colette wasn't an Institute student. She was of no interest to her.

Near to Colette, a long trestle-table had been laid with a fine range of sandwiches and snacks, prepared by Miss Radclyffe, the housekeeper at Fetch House, who was standing behind the table. Morgan smiled a secret smile to Radclyffe, and then continued with her introduction to the New Dawn.

'The New Dawn offers us all a chance to discover our true and hidden potential,' she told them. 'It gives the opportunity to order the world in the way it should be, in the way we want it, for the benefit of ourselves and for others.'

'And how do you do that?' asked Calvin Charles, as he munched on a ham and cheese roll.

'How often have you been faced with opposition from those who aren't as intelligent as yourselves?' Morgan asked. 'How often have people laughed at you, or made things awkward just because they're jealous of you?'

'Loads of times,' Marc muttered in the front row.

He remembered the tough time that Sergeant Ashby had once given him down in Brentmouth village. He'd only run an amber light on his bicycle, for heaven's sake, but Ashby had treated him like he'd just gone and murdered batty old Miss Rumford down at Rowan Cottage. Ashby had always held a grudge against the Institute students. So had lots of the other villagers, come to think of it.

'Exactly,' Morgan continued. 'They don't possess the intelligence to understand that the Institute students are different, superior. It is not they who should be making the rules, but you.'

'We're all of us superior to the rest of the country, to the rest of the world. It is our destiny to rule the weaker ones in society, show them the error of their ways.'

'And what if they don't want to be ruled?' Rebecca called out from the back of the hall. 'What do you do then?'

Morgan's mouth set firmly as she gazed challengingly at Rebecca. 'Then we impose that will on them,' she said plainly, and there was a small murmur of agreement from some of the students in the common room. 'They are weak of purpose, infirm in mind. They must be helped.'

'Maybe they don't want to be helped, like Rebecca says.' This was from Griff.

'People sometimes have to do things they don't

want to,' Morgan said. 'Take those missiles that even now are on their way to the Institute.'

'That's different,' Griff said, awkwardly. To cover his discomfort, he popped a barbecued chicken wing into his mouth.

'Is it?' Morgan asked slyly. 'The Government wants the missiles to pass by the Institute. So do General Axford and Eva and most of the teaching staff. But you say they're wrong. And so you're going to try and stop it. You're going to impose your will – your *superior* will – on them. You're going to make them do something they don't want. You are going to prove to them who is the real master around here.

'And if they refuse to bow to our will, then they must be stamped out,' Morgan concluded. 'They are not like us. They are *unlike*. And if they do not conform to our desires, then they must be cast out.'

'That's fascism,' Rebecca cried out from the back.

'No, it is the basis of a well-ordered society,' came back Morgan's ready reply.

'And that's what the New Dawn is all about?' Colette spoke up for the first time.

'You are not an Institute student: you wouldn't understand,' Morgan said, with barely-disguised contempt. 'We offer those who aren't as gifted as ourselves a continued and ordered existence under our guidance.'

'And those who don't agree get "cast out", I suppose,' Rebecca said scornfully. 'That's no better than what Hitler or any other dictator down the ages has done.'

'It's the foundation stone for a perfect world,' Morgan argued. 'Look at the wars in the world today. Look at the border disputes threatening to escalate into all-out conflicts. Only a few months ago, China and Zhou-zhun were on the brink of nuclear war. With people like ourselves in charge then there would be no more war, no more famine . . .'

Rebecca turned to Colette. 'C'mon, I don't want to hear any more of this rubbish,' she said, and declined the chicken salad sandwich that Radclyffe was offering her. 'We've got a party to get ready for.'

'Goodbye, Rebecca and your friend,' Morgan called out, as the two of them left the room. 'You may not agree with us, but the time of the New Dawn will come.'

'Yeah, but not if I can do anything about it,' Rebecca muttered. As she left she spotted Eva in the corner of the room. Rebecca frowned. She was certain that Eva had not been there when she and Colette had entered. And they had been standing by the door all the time. So, how had Eva got in the room?

That, however, wasn't the reason for Rebecca's concern. There was a curious expression on Eva's face, an expression that she couldn't ever remember having seen before.

For the first time since Rebecca had known her, Eva seemed actually to be frightened.

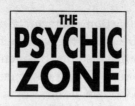

THE PSYCHIC ZONE

4

Party-time

Dateline: Study Bedroom C102, The Institute;
Wednesday 13 January; 19:15.

Liv Farrar looked up as the door to her bedroom opened and Rebecca and Colette both walked in. Liv, a Sixth Form computer studies student, was a popular girl. She was sitting at her Apple Mac, laying out the pages of the next edition of *The Enquirer*, which was due to be printed early next week. Scraps of paper and computer disks were scattered on the desk before her.

'Hi, you two,' she said. She closed the file she was working on, and then stood up from the desk to greet her two friends. She saw the two carrier bags which Rebecca and Colette were carrying from the most fashionable store in town and her face fell.

Rebecca and Colette didn't notice the look on Liv's

face, as Rebecca threw herself and her bag on to Liv's bed and Colette went over to see what Liv was working on.

'This is really cool of you, Liv,' Rebecca said, 'letting us change here. I'd hate to have to come all the way from the village in my party clothes. Ever since I gave up living on-site at the Institute and moved back in with Mom, it's such a drag having to come all the way in to school every morning. I really appreciate you letting us crash out here tonight after the party.'

'Er, yes . . . sure . . .' Liv said.

'Is there anything wrong, Liv?' Rebecca asked. 'It is still OK for us to stay here tonight, isn't it? I'm sure that even someone like Eva wouldn't want us to be walking home in the dark after the party.'

'Yes, of course it's all right for you to stay the night,' Liv said. She started to run her fingers through her short dark hair, the way she always did when she was nervous about something.

'What are you working on?' Colette asked, and tentatively moved the mouse of Liv's Apple Mac.

'The next issue of *The Enquirer*,' Liv replied, grateful for the change of subject. She reached over, double-clicked on one of the icons, and the front page of the newspaper appeared on the screen. 'It's nearly all finished,' she told them. 'All I need is a piece on the missile protest from Griff–'

'The General won't like that,' Rebecca said. She was still worried about Axford's threat to her if she didn't do something to halt Griff's demonstration.

'Then he can lump it,' Liv said, cheerfully. She had

a great reputation for not taking any nonsense from anyone. There'd even been a little bit of unease about the piece she'd written the other month about the Nazis' persecution of the Jews (too hard-hitting and why did she want to rake up the past, someone had said, but she'd run it all the same). 'And the other piece is Marc's interview with my dear friend, Morgan Knight.'

'You don't like her, I take it?' asked Colette, who had noted the sarcastic tone in Liv's voice.

'How do you know that?'

'Just call me psychic,' she said, and shared a smile with Rebecca at the private joke.

'You're right,' Liv agreed. 'I first met her on a study trip to the States a couple of years ago. She was a really nice girl, if a little bit gawky and self-conscious. Now take a look at her.'

'I see what you mean,' Rebecca said. 'She's changed – and how!'

'Maybe it's all something to do with this New Dawn nonsense,' Liv said, as she clicked through the pages of *The Enquirer* on-screen.

'You know something about it?' Rebecca wanted to know.

'Just fragments I've picked up through reading the international press,' Liv said. 'Maybe I'll do a piece on it next issue. It was started three-and-a-bit years ago by Annie Ward.'

'Who?'

'You know, the woman who made headlines for being the first woman to come within a few thousand kilometres of Mars in the *Deimos I* spacecraft. She started up the New Dawn movement. Sounds just like a nutty cult, that's all. You get 'em two-a-penny in the States these days.'

'You wouldn't say that if you'd've been at the meeting today,' Colette said.

'Funny though,' Liv said, as she carried on working her way through the on-screen pages. She reached a blank page, the one on which Marc's interview was scheduled to appear. 'Morgan never showed any interest in organised religion before. Neither did her dad, come to think of it . . .'

'What's happened?' Colette asked, as she watched Liv click frantically on her mouse.

'Blasted thing's frozen on me *again*!' Liv said through gritted teeth. She pressed the reboot switch on the Mac and the screen went blank.

'It's happened before?' Colette enquired.

'Three times today,' Liv said. 'And twice yesterday.'

'Could the file be corrupted?' Rebecca asked.

'No,' Liv said. 'And I ran a virus check as well. Nothing. If I didn't know better then I'd say it was some sort of outside influence.'

Rebecca immediately thought of the impressive array of computer equipment she and Joey had found in Johnny Lau's room. The Apple Mac buzzed back into life and Liv opened up her file. It seemed to be working perfectly now, she noticed.

Colette, who understood very little about computers, changed the subject. She yawned for effect.

'Come on, you two,' she said. 'Let's get ourselves ready for the party.'

'Ah, I wanted to speak to you about that,' Liv said.

'There *is* something wrong, isn't there?' Colette said.

Liv nodded. 'You can't come,' she told her.

'Why not?'

'Christina said that only Institute students can come to her party,' Liv said. 'I'm sorry...'

'But that's crazy,' Rebecca protested. 'She told me only this morning that Colette could come along. Any friend of mine was a friend of hers, she said.'

Liv looked even more embarrassed, if that was at all possible. 'The thing is, *you* can't come either, Rebecca.'

'Come off it!' she snapped. 'I'm one of Christina's best pals.'

'But you don't live on-site anymore,' Liv explained. 'There's been a change of plan. Now it's only for Institute students who live in one of the two hostels.'

'I bet that Morgan Knight is going and she doesn't live on-site,' said Colette.

'Look, I really am sorry, you two, Liv said, 'but that's what she told me to tell you.'

Rebecca gritted her teeth and there was a determined look on her face. 'So we're banned from Christina's party, are we?'

''Fraid so,' replied Liv.

'Well, we'll see about that!'

Dateline: Study Bedroom B331, The Institute;
Wednesday 13 January; 19:15.

'So, where were you last night?' Joey asked Marc when he met him, as arranged, in the boys' hostel at the same time that Rebecca and Colette were turning up to see Liv.

Marc looked up from his PC, where he had just started typing up the interview with Morgan Knight. He still hadn't got round to it. In fact, if the truth was to be known, he'd forgotten that he had a deadline on it. That was kind of worrying him: perhaps he was growing absent-minded in his old age!

'What d'you mean?' he asked. There was a worried look on his face, just as if Joey had touched on a subject which he didn't want to discuss.

Joey grinned. 'Well, we all know that you weren't helping Christina with her party last night,' Joey said, and winked at Marc. 'So you stayed behind at Fetch House with Morgan, eh? Marc, my man, I'm proud of you.'

Marc scowled. 'Look, Joey, what's it to you where I was last night?' he asked, angrily. He stabbed at one of the keys on his keyboard. His PC seemed to have crashed on him again. It had been the third time it had happened during his writing of the article.

Joey was taken aback by his friend's reaction. He raised his hands up in a disarming gesture.

'Hey, chill out, big buddy,' he said. 'I didn't mean nothing with it.'

'Well, just keep your nose out of my private business, will you?' Marc barked back.

He smashed his fist on his desk. The PC wasn't responding to any of his attempts to unfreeze it. Had he been screwing up again? He'd been forgetting more and more things lately, he realised. Just little things, sure, but added together . . . It was probably stress. After all, he had been working harder than usual, what with trying to catch up on his grades and all that.

He pressed the reboot button, just as Liv had done in the girls' hostel. The article blipped off-screen.

'Look, I was congratulating you, that's all,' Joey said, defensively. Marc's outburst was only making his seemingly interminable headache worse.

'What makes you think that a kid like you has the right to criticise what I've been doing?'

Joey was perplexed. 'Criticising? Hey, I sure wasn't – Hey, whaddya mean? "A kid like me"?' he asked. *Jeez!* he thought. *Am I ever having a headache!*

'Well, look at you,' Marc said. 'You come over here to England and start acting like you own the place. What's so special about you? You're good at maths and you can perform a couple of parlour tricks. So what?'

'So my parlour tricks have helped you out of a couple of dodgy situations in the past,' Joey retaliated. 'And as for math, Doctor Molloy said that I was one of the best students she'd ever known.'

'Doctor Molloy!' Marc laughed scornfully. 'She was always a soft touch. She probably only dragged you off the streets 'cos she took pity on you!'

The comment hurt Joey to the core. His fists clenched and unclenched, but he tried to restrain himself from hitting Marc. 'Pity? What do you mean by that?'

'You really think a slum kid like you deserves to be at the Institute?'

'Just as much as you do, buster,' Joey said. Marc was asking for a fight, and if he carried on in this way then he was sure as hell going to get it.

'Don't compare me with you,' Marc said. 'I was born and raised in this country. Not like you. You're *unlike*. You should go back and fester in your New York gutter with the rest of your good-for-nothing nigger friends.'

Joey saw red. He had fought all his life against racism and he wasn't prepared to put up with it from a guy whom he regarded as his best buddy. His head was burning now, not with a headache, but with pure uncontrolled hatred. He tensed his body, ready to spring on to Marc and beat him to the ground if needs be. Marc was ready too and his body was shaking with rage and with anger.

And then Joey stopped. No, he wasn't going to resort to violence, he told himself. What good would that do to that limey scumbag he used to call his friend? He shook his head.

'You know something, Marc,' he said, with some sadness in his voice. 'I used to call you my best buddy. Now you're just pathetic. See you around, loser.'

And, trying to keep as much dignity as possible,

Joey turned and left Marc's room, slamming the door as he went.

Joey stood outside the door for several seconds, breathing hard and trying to control his temper. He started to see things more clearly. Why had Marc suddenly turned on him like that?

He almost raised a hand to knock on Marc's door and ask to be let in again. Instead, he did one of the things he most hated. He tried to enter the mind of a friend.

Joey screwed up his eyes and concentrated, beaming all his thoughts into Marc's room, trying to make some sort of contact with the older boy's own thoughts, attempting to read his mind and to see what was wrong. He could do it easily enough with Colette, who shared some of his ESP talents, but it was something he'd never tried before with Marc.

Nothing. Joey concentrated even harder, trying to ignore the headache which was making the veins at his temples pulse fiercely.

Still nothing. Joey couldn't make any kind of connection with Marc. Resigning himself to failure, Joey walked off down the corridor.

If Joey *had* been able to read Marc's thoughts, he would have wondered why Marc was now sitting at his desk, his head in his hands, crying his heart out. He was realising that he had just said the most evil things to his best mate, things which ought never to be forgiven. Marc didn't know what was wrong with him lately – he was really losing his grip; even starting to forget important things, like the deadline for *The Enquirer* piece, for instance. He had no clear idea of where he had been last night, either. All he could remember was a brick in his hands and flames, as they licked out of a third floor window.

Dateline: The Assembly Hall, The Institute;
Wednesday 13 January; 21.14.

By the time Rebecca and Colette arrived at the Assembly Hall, which was in its own separate building in the Institute grounds, Christina Haack's party was in full swing. Even from the girls' hostel they could hear the sound of the latest dance CDs and the chilly January air was hot with expectation. Christina's parties were almost legendary at the Institute and, from the sound of the music and the trendily-dressed students milling around the entrance, it looked as if this one was going to be no exception.

'Do you think this is a good idea, Rebecca?' Colette asked warily as they approached the large Gothic building.

'Of course it is,' Rebecca said, and glanced nervously at the two bouncers on the door. She recognised them as two boys from the Upper Sixth who spent all of their spare time playing rugby. 'You and I were invited to this party and we are going to go, whether Christina Haack likes it or not!'

'It *is* her party after all,' Colette said. 'She has a right to invite who she wants.'

'And she should also stick to her promises,' Rebecca said self-righteously, as she approached the two bouncers.

Glancing past them through the wide-open double doors she could see that the party was in full swing. Griff was there, she noticed, together with Marc and Calvin Charles. If she'd taken a longer look she would have been surprised to see that Joey was absent and also that – contrary to what Joey had said – Johnny Lau was there, chatting away to Morgan Knight (around whom, of course, most of the boys were hovering). She would also have seen Liv Farrar there, who was keeping a discreet distance from her former friend.

Rebecca attempted a cheery smile at the two bouncers, Andrew and Kevin, whom she knew vaguely. They might have been built like burly rugby players, but she remembered them as really kind and easy-going guys. She'd even had a crush on Kevin once, much to his own girlfriend's distress.

'Hi, guys,' she said. She had to raise her voice a little to make herself heard above the sound of the heavy nose-bleed techno music coming from inside the hall.

'Hi, Rebecca,' Kevin said, and nodded a hello to Colette as well. 'What can we do for you?'

'Let us in, will you?' Rebecca asked. 'I want to party.'

Kevin shook his head and Andrew took a menacing

step towards the two girls. 'Sorry, Rebecca,' Kevin said. 'You know I can't do that.'

'Of course you can,' Rebecca said briskly, and started to push her way past the two boys. Kevin restrained her with a heavy hand. His fingers pressed hard into her shoulder.

'Hey, get your hands off me,' she said, and Kevin did so. He wouldn't let her pass, however.

'Rebecca, I think we'd better go,' Colette said.

'Rubbish,' Rebecca said, petulantly, and stamped her foot. 'C'mon, you guys, Christina invited us to her party.'

Andrew shook his head. 'Well, now she's *un*invited you, is that clear?' he said. 'She doesn't want your sort around here.'

'My sort?'

'You know what I mean,' he said.

'No, I don't.'

'Is there something the matter, boys?' came Christina's voice. She walked up behind the two bouncers.

'Storm won't leave,' Kevin said to Christina. 'I told her that we don't want her sort at your party.'

'Christina, this has gone beyond a joke,' Rebecca said angrily. 'You invited us this morning. What's happened? Why does Liv reckon that you've gone and changed your mind? Let us in, will you?'

'Like Kevin said, we don't want your sort in here,' Christina said. There was an icy tone to her voice, almost as cold as the January wind which was howling outside the hall.

'For heaven's sake, what do you mean, "my sort".'

'I thought your sort would have learnt your lesson back in Berlin,' Christina remarked. 'Obviously you didn't.'

'Back in Berlin?' Rebecca said. 'I've never been to Germany in my life. Sure, Dad's family came from there in the forties and they had to leave when . . .'

The penny finally dropped for Rebecca. She felt her whole body start to quake with anger and revulsion. She thought that the horrors of the Nazi concentration camps had put paid to this sort of prejudice. She was obviously wrong.

'You're saying I can't come in here because I'm Jewish?' she gasped.

'*I* didn't say that,' Christina said, and looked at the two boys. 'Did I say that, guys?'

'I didn't hear you saying it, Christina,' Kevin said.

'Nor did I,' agreed Andrew.

Rebecca felt the bile rise in her throat and the anger in her breast. She lifted a hand to strike Christina, but Kevin caught her wrist in his firm grasp.

'Face it, Rebecca,' Christina said. 'We don't want your type here.'

'You're . . . you're nothing but a filthy Nazi!' Rebecca said, seeing her German friend in her true light for the first time. She struggled to free herself from Kevin's grasp. 'And I'm surprised – no, *disgusted* at you two.'

By this time a small group, attracted by all the commotion, had gathered behind Andrew and Kevin. Rebecca kicked Kevin on the shin and when he slapped her across the face no one seemed prepared to help. Someone cheered.

'That's right,' Calvin Charles snarled. 'Teach her some manners. Teach her some respect.'

Colette came to Rebecca's aid and managed to free her from Kevin. It was all in vain, however, as Andrew grabbed hold of her. There was an evil, lustful look in his eyes and Colette knew that he was capable of anything.

She struggled in his grip, hoping against hope for someone to come and help them. The crowd cheered them on. By now the crowd was so large that no one inside the hall would have been able to see them.

'Go on!' someone said. 'Teach those cows a lesson! Give 'em what they deserve.'

Instinctively, Colette closed her eyes. *Joey! Joey! Please help us!* she called out with her mind. There was no reply.

And then help came from the most unexpected quarter.

'I say, what's going on?' came a croaky voice from behind Rebecca and Colette. An old frail-looking man, dressed in a shabby tweed jacket and trousers and walking with a cane, was approaching them.

'What's it look like, grandad? We're teaching these two a lesson they'll never forget.'

'I was just leaving the chemistry labs when I heard all this noise,' Mr Skinner, the chemistry teacher, said and then peered through his *pince-nez* spectacles at Rebecca and Colette. 'I say, are you two girls in any sort of trouble?'

'Please help us,' Colette pleaded. There were tears streaming down her face now, as Andrew increased his hold on her arm. It was almost as if he was enjoying the pain he was inflicting on her.

Although over sixty and fading fast, Ted Skinner was no coward. He raised his cane threateningly at Kevin and Andrew. 'Leave them alone!' he cried out, in a voice which was quaking more with old age than with fear. 'Or I'll have to stop you!'

'Yeah?' asked Calvin, who was bashing his fist into the palm of his other hand, plainly itching for a fight. 'You and whose army?'

Kevin and Andrew released Rebecca and Colette, and shoved them to the ground. Licking their lips, they advanced on Mr Skinner.

They struck the old man to the ground and started kicking him in the side. The others crowded in on them, and one of them wrenched his walking stick from his hand and started to bash him over the head with it.

Rebecca and Colette picked themselves up. They could no longer see Mr Skinner now. He was surrounded by the crowd of attackers. They could hear him cry out in agony, as he was kicked and punched and thumped. Rebecca didn't know which was worse: Skinner's cries, or the whoops of laughter from the thugs.

They looked at Morgan Knight, who was standing by the doors. She had closed them so that Griff or Johnny or Marc or anyone else wouldn't see what was going on and come to their aid.

She was smiling maniacally and there was an almost ecstatic beam on her face, as she watched her friends brutally beat up the old teacher.

'We have to get help,' Rebecca said.

'*We* must help him,' Colette protested.

'We can't do it alone!' Rebecca said. She started running off in the direction of the girls' hostel and Colette followed. 'We can phone the police from there.'

But as Rebecca ran to find a phone, she knew in her heart that any help they could get now for Mr Skinner would be way too late in coming. At the thought of his heroism she felt a lump in her throat, and had to fight hard to hold back her tears.

Morgan Knight watched them go and made no attempt to follow them. Let them phone the police if they wanted. Even if they could have done – and she knew that they couldn't – it was already too late.

It had been too late for over nine months. From the twenty-sixth of March, in fact, when Armstrong Knight had first floated in the interplanetary space between Earth and Mars.

Dateline: Study bedroom C102, The Institute;
Wednesday 13 January; 21:14.

'Come on,' Colette urged, as Rebecca searched through the pockets of her dress for the swipe card which would open the main door to the girls' hostel. When she had stopped living on-site, she should have handed the card in. Now she was glad that she hadn't.

Finally she found the card, quickly ran it through the reader, and rushed into the entrance hall. She glanced quickly behind them. No one was following them.

She ran to the bank of payphones at the far end of the room and picked up the receiver of the first one. Like the others, it was connected to the Institute's main switchboard and she would first of all have to dial nine for an outside line before inserting her money. (The General and Eva liked to know precisely who their students kept in regular contact with.)

Rebecca's face fell. There was no dialling tone. She tried each of the others in turn. They were all dead.

'Do you have a mobile on you?' she asked Colette.

'Of course not,' she replied. 'Why would I want to take it to Christina's party?'

Rebecca thought hard for a moment. Most of the hostel's occupants were at Christina's party, so there was no point in knocking on any of their doors to see if anyone possessed a portable phone.

'Liv Farrar!' she realised suddenly, and produced the key which Liv had lent her. 'She's got a mobile!'

They raced up the three flights of stairs – for some reason the lift wasn't working – and into Liv's room, not bothering to turn on the light. The moon coming in from the open window was good enough for them to see by. Rebecca picked up Liv's portable phone and punched out nine-nine-nine. She turned to Colette. Even in the moonlight Colette could see just how worried she was.

'It's dead as well,' she said.

'But how?'

There was no time to wonder. Rebecca went over to Liv's desk.

'What are you doing?' Colette asked.

'Liv's got a modem which she uses for sending last-minute copy for *The Enquirer* to the printer's,' Rebecca said. 'If we can just get out an E-mail we can . . .'

Her voice tailed off. In the moonlight she could see that the Apple Mac's screen had been smashed. The keyboard had been covered in something wet and sticky. It smelt like paint. Colette crossed over to the open doorway and flicked on the light.

'Is the whole Institute going crazy?' Rebecca asked, and then heard Colette asking her to turn around. Rebecca did so. What she saw made her almost physically sick with revulsion.

Someone had been in Liv Farrar's room while they had all been out. For, daubed on the wall, in red paint the colour of blood, were words which literally struck terror into Rebecca's heart. The letters read:

JEW-FRIENDS OUT.
KEEP THE INSTITUTE PURE.
CAST OUT THE UNLIKE!

Rebecca shuddered. She remembered the tales her gran had told her of Nazi Germany. Of how even friends and supporters of Jews were hounded just as much as the Jews themselves. Someone must have seen her visit Liv's room earlier and remembered Liv's

Enquirer article of a few issues ago about the Nazi persecution of the Jews. That would have branded her as scum in their perverted eyes.

Things at the Institute were getting way out of control.

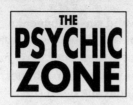

THE PSYCHIC ZONE

5

The Morning After

Dateline: Fiveways;
Thursday 14 January; 07.30.

'That's sick,' Marc said when he turned up at Fiveways the following morning with Griff.

Rebecca had called him first thing to tell him about the horrific scene the night before, when Ted Skinner had been so brutally attacked, and about what had happened in Liv's room afterwards. She needn't have bothered. Liv had told Marc and he was already on his way to Fiveways, where Rebecca had stayed that night in Colette's spare room. Griff had offered to drive him over in the car his father had bought him for his seventeenth birthday last September after he'd passed his driving test.

'And you're sure you didn't see anything?' Rebecca asked. She was still shaken by the series of events of the night before and she no longer knew who to trust. She had thought that Kevin and Andrew and Calvin had all been good friends of hers, but they had all turned on her and poor Mr Skinner, nearly beating him to death. Could she be so sure of Marc?

'Of course not,' Marc retorted. 'Do you think I would let something like that happen to someone as defenceless as old Skinner – or that I wouldn't have come to *your* rescue?'

'No,' said Rebecca, wondering why she was relieved at Marc's admission. Of course Marc hadn't seen anything.

'The doors were closed,' Marc said. 'Liv mentioned the fact to me. She said that it was hot with all those people dancing and she wished we could have had some more ventilation. You should have been there, Bec! I tell you, it was one of the best parties ever.'

'Convenient that, wasn't it?' Colette said. Rebecca and Marc both turned to her.

'What are you saying, Colette?' Marc asked. His manner was cool and calm. Didn't he realise the danger that she and Rebecca had been in? Colette wondered.

'Nothing,' Colette replied. She continued to stare at Marc, until he found it uncomfortable.

'For God's sake, Marc, I nearly got killed there!' Rebecca said, finally no longer able to control her temper.

'It was a little misunderstanding, that's all,' Marc said.

'Marc, Christina made some racist remarks about me!' Rebecca reminded him.

'What did she actually say?' he asked her. 'Did she say that you were being excluded from the party because of the fact that you were Jewish?'

Rebecca paused. 'Well, no, not exactly . . .' she finally admitted.

'Well, there you have it,' Marc said, and smiled. He reached over and patted Rebecca's knee in a friendly manner. Rebecca swatted it away: as far as she was concerned, it was in a patronising manner. 'Christina is the least racist person I know.'

'Oh yes?' asked Colette, as she continued to scrutinise Marc with her eyes. 'That's not how it seemed last night.'

'Johnny Lau was there last night and he's Chinese,' Marc said, and leant back in his chair and crossed his legs. 'And so was Loomali Nadau: he's from Nairobi in Kenya. *And* Yvonne Jirwullur–'

'Who?' The name meant nothing to Rebecca or to Colette.

'She's an Aborigine who won a scholarship to come to the Institute and study maths.'

'Oh, *her*,' said Rebecca who studied maths subsid herself. 'I've seen her around. Never thought to ask her name. She didn't look like my sort of person . . .'

'Now who's being racist?' Marc asked, pointedly. He leant forward in his chair and uncrossed his legs. 'And then that's not to mention Abe Cohen, who's about as Jewish as they come! Bec, that party last night was like the United Nations on a good day. No way can you say that Christina was being racist.'

'It happened none the less,' said Colette, sticking up for Rebecca and still keeping her eyes on Marc. He shifted uneasily in his chair.

Marc leant even further forward and started twiddling his thumbs. 'Bec, you've got totally the wrong end of the stick,' he said, sounding sincere. 'Christina managed to talk the local cops into turning a blind eye if alcohol was served on the premises. Nothing too strong – just some bottled beers and a couple of wine boxes. But the condition the police made was that everyone who went to the party had to live on-site. That's why you and Colette weren't allowed in. That's the only reason.'

For a moment Colette seemed to believe Marc, until Colette said, 'We saw Morgan there. She doesn't live on-site.'

'Morgan can do what she wants,' Marc said, automatically and without thinking.

'Can she now?'

Marc turned away. Wouldn't Colette ever stop looking at him with those accusing eyes of hers?

'Yes, she can,' he replied. 'You're not an Institute student. You wouldn't understand things like that. You're unlike us . . .'

Unlike . . .

The word which had been scrawled on Liv Farrar's wall. The word that had been scribbled on the racist message thrown through Johnny Lau's window. The word Morgan Knight had used at her meeting in the

Junior Common Room. Rebecca and Colette both shuddered.

Just then the door opened and Griff walked in. Colette smiled when she saw him. He had been on the phone in the other room to the Brentmouth Cottage Hospital. Mr Skinner was in a critical condition, he told them. He had suffered some broken bones and was still unconscious. He was also in an oxygen tent at the moment, on account of his age, but the doctors seemed to think that he wouldn't die from his injuries.

'They say that the police reckon there's hardly any chance of catching the scum,' he told them. 'There's been a lot of muggings in the area recently.'

'It wasn't a mugging,' Rebecca insisted.

'We've only your and Colette's word for that,' Marc said gently. 'Against the word of Christina and Andrew and Kevin and Calvin. They saw nothing. When the police had arrived, they'd just found him unconscious and bleeding on the ground outside the hall.'

'But . . .' Rebecca began, and then stopped. She knew that it was no use arguing with Marc. Either he really was convinced that she and Colette had imagined all that had happened last night, or he was lying and Morgan Knight had him under some sort of power. She decided to maintain her silence for the moment.

Marc stood up to leave. 'If you're sure you're OK, then I'll be off,' he said. He looked at Griff. 'You OK to drive me back to the Institute, mate?'

'Sure,' Griff said, and then added: 'but on one condition.'

'Which is?'

'That we stop off at that new burger joint on the way,' he said. 'I could murder a cheeseburger with fries!'

'You eat meat?' Colette asked. 'I thought that you'd be a veggie like Rebecca here.'

Griff looked sheepish. 'Ah, well, yes . . . I used to be,' he admitted. 'But I sort of, well, lapsed. You won't tell anyone, will you, Colette? It'd do my reputation as the Institute's friendly neighbourhood all-round good guy and eco-warrior no good at all, would it!'

'OK,' Colette said. 'I promise.'

'Great, then that's settled,' Marc said. 'Only I've got a better idea. Instead of paying over the odds for a cheeseburger, let's eat at the Institute. The food's much better now that Ma Chapman and her stodge menu have gone.'

'OK, Marc, it's a deal,' he said, and slapped his pal on the back. He looked at the girls. 'You coming?' he asked them.

'No,' said Colette. 'We've both eaten at home.'

'Besides, we've other things to do before classes start,' Rebecca said.

'We have?'

'Yes,' said Rebecca, and waved the two boys goodbye.

'He was lying,' Colette said, as soon as Marc and Griff had gone.

'Who? Marc?' asked Rebecca. 'What have you been doing? "Zapping" him, like Joey does?'

'I don't have to read his mind,' Colette said. 'His

body language was all wrong. He was fidgeting so much in his chair that he had to be not telling the truth.'

'Well, we'll soon find out,' Rebecca said.

'How?'

'The Institute is covered by closed-circuit cameras twenty-four hours a day,' Rebecca told her. 'It was one of Eva's ideas. The attack on us and Mr Skinner will have been recorded on video. We'll soon prove whether we imagined what happened or not.'

'That's great,' said Colette, and then wondered why Rebecca wasn't showing any signs of getting up and going. 'What are you waiting for?'

'Nothing,' Rebecca said. 'But there's something I have to do first.'

'Then, let's get going,' Colette said eagerly.

'Not you,' Rebecca said. 'This is something only Joey can help me with.'

'Joey?' asked Colette. 'Where is he? I tried to call out for him last night when we were being attacked. I couldn't reach him. That's never happened to me before. I've always had a vague idea where he was. Why hasn't he come to see how we both are? I'd've thought that he would have come down with Marc and Griff.'

'Maybe he hasn't heard the news yet?'

'Or maybe Marc hasn't told him,' Colette said.

'Then I'll have to phone him at the Institute,' Rebecca said. 'He and I are going to visit Morgan Knight at Fetch House. We're going to find out exactly what's going on!'

Dateline: Fetch House;
Thursday 14 January; 09.45.

Rebecca rapped smartly on the door of Fetch House and, while she was waiting for a reply, looked around at her surroundings.

Like Marc, Rebecca thought that Fetch House seemed a rather odd address for Armstrong Knight to choose as his daughter's home in England. It was located miles away from anywhere and she guessed that it would take a good three-quarters of an hour to get from here to the Institute. The only thing which Rebecca thought would be of even the vaguest interest to someone like Morgan, would be the Fetch Hill radio-telescope to the north.

Finally the door creaked open and Morgan was standing there in the open doorway. She seemed surprised to see Rebecca, but nevertheless smiled.

'And what have I done to deserve this pleasure?' she asked, in a voice which oozed sarcasm and insincerity.

'You know exactly what,' Rebecca said, and pushed her way past and into the cottage.

'You're trespassing, you know,' Morgan said. 'I could call the police. It's a criminal offence.'

'And so's racism and beating up defenceless old men.'

'Skinner is still alive?' Morgan sounded surprised.

'So you admit it then?' Rebecca asked. 'You admit that your thugs nearly killed him last night?'

'I'm admitting nothing,' Morgan said. 'All I heard was that poor Mr Skinner got attacked by a gang of muggers last night in the Institute grounds. It was probably some blacks or some Jews. You can never trust them, you know.'

Rebecca saw red but persuaded herself not to reach out and strike Morgan. That wasn't the intelligent way to deal with her kind of racism, though she knew that it would feel good. She forced herself to keep cool although, inside, she was burning up with anger.

'I'm surprised the Institute isn't better guarded,' Morgan continued. 'After all, the world's elite must be protected from the rest of the population.'

Rebecca glowered at her. 'The Institute *is* protected,' she said. 'We have a state-of-the-art security system throughout the grounds. The gates can be locked at a moment's notice and even the barbed wire and railings at the perimeter walls can be electrified when the General or Eva decides.'

'I know,' Morgan said, and Rebecca wondered exactly how it was that she did know. The new security measures had been introduced by Eva only about nine months ago. Her excuse had been that a band of local hooligans had climbed over the walls and vandalised one of the labs, the consequence of which was the explosion which had lost General Axford the use of his legs. The vandals had never been caught, however.

'But is that to keep the outside scum away – or keep some scum in so that they can be better controlled and won't corrupt the rest of the community?' Morgan asked.

'Is that supposed to refer to me?' Rebecca said, and again resisted the temptation to hit Morgan.

'Did I say that?' Morgan asked, sweetly.

Rebecca ignored her. 'But what you probably don't know is that the grounds are also covered by closed-circuit cameras. Everything which happens at the Institute is recorded on video.'

'That must be very handy for Eva,' Morgan remarked.

'What do you mean?' Rebecca asked.

'Have you never wondered who she is?' Morgan asked.

'No,' Rebecca lied, uncertain what Morgan was talking about. Of course she'd wondered who Eva really was. Of course she'd wondered what secrets lay beneath those dark glasses of hers. 'Tell me.'

Morgan refused to answer. Instead, she sighed with relief. 'It feels so good that those muggers will be caught,' she said. 'At least Mr Skinner will be grateful when they are brought to justice. Which hospital did you say they'd taken him to?'

'Brentmouth Cottage Hospital,' Rebecca said, before she'd had a chance to realise that she hadn't already told Morgan where the chemistry teacher had been sent to last night when the ambulance had finally arrived.

'Then I must order him some flowers,' Morgan said. 'Daddy always taught me to look after people less fortunate than myself.'

'Yeah, I bet he did,' Rebecca said sarcastically. 'Bully them, more like. Just as you've bullied Marc.'

'Marc Price? Is he your boyfriend then?'

'No.'

'Then why are you so concerned about him?'

'He's my best friend,' Rebecca said. 'And ever since you've been at the Institute he's changed somehow.' She remembered Marc's racist comments and his unwillingness to help either the black Joey or the Chinese Johnny Lau. That hadn't been the Marc that she'd known for so long.

'Then maybe he's seen the light,' Morgan said. 'The light of the New Dawn.'

'No.' Rebecca was certain about that. 'I hate all cults, whether it's the New Dawn or any other organisation that tries to prove that it's superior to everyone else.'

'Maybe Marc disagrees,' Morgan said, and added with a deliberately superior smile: 'after all, one man's meat is another man's poison . . .'

'I don't know what you mean.'

'Your type never do.'

Just then the door to the living-room opened and Radclyffe stepped in. This was the first time that Rebecca had seen her close up, other than at the New Dawn meeting when she had been serving the sandwiches and refreshments. Like Marc before her, Rebecca wondered where she had seen her face before.

'Now,' said Radclyffe, 'how may we help you?'

THE PSYCHIC ZONE

6

The New Dawn Breaks

Dateline: Fetch House;
Thursday 14 January; 09.55.

While Rebecca was being confronted by Morgan and her housekeeper with the oddly-familiar face, Joey had sneaked around the back of Fetch House.

The door was locked, but that posed no problems whatsoever for him. He'd been breaking and entering ever since he'd been a little kid.

He entered the kitchen. Nothing out of the ordinary there, he thought, as he made his way to a door which, he guessed, led to the cellar. He rattled the handle. That was locked as well. No problem there either, or so he thought. He took the twisted piece of wire which he always carried in the pocket of his baseball jacket and wiggled it about in the lock.

No result. He tried again.

The door refused to open.

He looked up and recognised the electronic lock which was set high up in the door, which could be only released by punching out the correct numbers on the digital keyboard there.

Joey chuckled to himself. This was even easier! he thought. With his psychic powers he'd be able to suss out the code in half the time it took him to break a conventional lock. Heck, even Colette had done the same thing once before when they'd been vacationing in London and she had to break into a safe. If a limey like Colette could do it then so could he!

Joey closed his eyes, reached up his hand, and touched the electronic lock. He emptied his mind of everything but the sensation of the cold metal on his fingers and tried to zero in on the correct combination which would release the locking mechanism.

Nothing. The exact same nothing he had felt when he'd tried to 'zap' into Johnny Lau's mind. The exact same big fat zero he'd felt when he'd attempted to link up with Marc after their argument.

Joey opened his eyes, and there was a worried look in them. Was he losing his touch? Or was it the effect of mixing with all those blasted, jumped-up limeys, those grown-ups like Eva and Axford and Skinner (who should really have died in that attack), and all those other foreigners? Those other foreigners like that damn slanty-eyed Johnny Lau, who he'd never trusted. Neither had Colette, so he knew that he must be right. Or that crazy Abo girl from Oz . . . what was her name? Yvonne Jirwullur or something? Yeah.

Something foreign, anyway. Something *unlike*. Why didn't people like her and that Abe Cohen Yid-guy realise that they didn't belong with guys like him? Why didn't they just go back and fester in the gutter with all the rest of their no-good friends?

Joey raised his hand to his brow. That headache was back. It was probably the fault of all those foreigners and outsiders anyway. All the fault of the *unlike*. Yeah, that was what it was. The unlike. They were to blame for everything.

Joey returned to the task in hand. He had to find out what Morgan and Radclyffe were up to. Even if Rebecca, the person who wanted him to do that, was an unlike herself. And, he found himself thinking, why should he help someone like Rebecca Storm anyway? Heck, if he had to choose, he'd side with Morgan Knight any day. After all, Rebecca was different. Rebecca Storm was *unlike* . . .

No! some voice sounded in Joey's head, clearing it for the moment. *Rebecca is my friend, my friend* . . .

Joey left the locked cellar door, found the backstairs, and climbed them. At the top of the landing there were just two doors, both of which were unlocked. He opened the first door.

This room obviously belonged to Radclyffe. He could tell that by the furnishings in the room and the old-fashioned clothes which had been draped over the chairs.

He went over to the bookshelf, just as that Jew-girl – *no*, he corrected himself sternly, as he struggled to fight the racism and hatred which was somehow struggling to take him over, *just as his friend, Rebecca* – just as his *friend*, Rebecca had told him to do.

Nothing out of the ordinary. A couple of cook books. No problem there. He guessed that Radclyffe did most of the cooking for Morgan: he remembered Calvin Charles telling him that Radclyffe had provided the sandwiches for Morgan's talk on the New Dawn at the Institute.

A couple of yukky romantic novels. Well, Radclyffe was a woman, after all, and everyone knew that you couldn't trust women, they were weak and selfish and deceitful and–

No! Joey thought. *Rebecca and Colette are two of my best friends and they're both female!*

No, there was nothing unusual on Radclyffe's bookshelf.

Apart from one thing, that was. A dusty volume, tattered and torn with age. Joey took it down from the shelf and read the title on its spine.

Life on Mars?

Joey chuckled. Life on Mars? Jeez. of course there wasn't life on Mars. Every kid knew that. Sure, maybe there had been years ago and, fair enough, there was still a case for bacteria existing beneath the dry and arid Martian surface. But intelligent life? No way. Not for uncountable millions of years at least.

He opened the book and flicked through its pages. A whole heap of pretentious and inaccurate rubbish, as he'd suspected. And then he looked at the title-page.

To Anne, the inscription read, *hoping you might*

find this as much fun as I did, Armstrong.

Armstrong. That was clearly Morgan's father, Joey realised. But who was Anne? And what was Radclyffe doing reading the book?

He shut the volume and replaced it on the shelf. Seeing that there was nothing else of any possible interest, he left the room and sneaked across the landing into what he rightly guessed was Morgan's room.

There was nothing of any particular interest there either. Just a stack of literature about the New Dawn (the usual stuff which he'd seen pinned up on the Institute noticeboard) and a pile of biology and chemistry textbooks, which was hardly surprising for a biology and chemistry whizzkid like Morgan.

Joey picked up one book entitled *The Human Brain*, a boring title for what seemed like an even more boring book. He scanned the contents pages and saw that one of the chapters was underlined. *Serotonin and Other Neurotransmitters.* The name rang a bell in his mind and he remembered Rebecca explaining the word to Johnny Lau. Serotonin was a chemical in the brain which altered a person's moods. What interest did that have for Morgan Knight?

He glanced at his watch. It was now almost ten o'clock. He didn't have much time left. Rebecca couldn't stall Morgan and Radclyffe downstairs forever. He'd have to leave before he was discovered. Cursing himself that he'd discovered absolutely nothing, Joey started to make his way back down the stairs.

Dateline: Fetch House;
Thursday 14 January; 10.00.

'I think you had better go now,' Radclyffe told Rebecca. Rebecca looked at her in amazement.

'You mean that you're not even interested that the person you're supposed to be looking after here was behind the beating up of an old man last night?' she asked.

'That is not the way of the New Dawn,' Radclyffe said. 'We believe in peaceful persuasion at all times.'

'Yeah, sure,' Rebecca said, and studied Radclyffe's face more closely than the older woman cared for. 'Do I know you from somewhere?'

'I doubt it,' she said. 'Now, either produce some evidence for your insubstantial and scurrilous accusations or I shall have no alternative but to call in the local police.'

'Oh, I'll produce the evidence, all right,' Rebecca said with determination, and turned to go. Morgan led her to the door.

'And if you can't produce your evidence then what will you do, dear Rebecca?' she asked. 'Fake it, like your kind did back in Berlin?'

Rebecca glared red-hot daggers at her. 'The others will back up my claim,' she stated.

'Others who supposedly beat up a poor old man?' Morgan's tone was sarcastic. 'You think they'd implicate themselves? It's all gone too far now.'

'Too far? What's gone too far?'

'You'll see soon enough,' she replied enigmatically, and shut the door in Rebecca's face.

When she had done so, Joey emerged from where he'd been hiding in the bushes by the cottage door. Rebecca looked enquiringly at him.

'Well?' she asked.

'Nothing,' Joey said. 'Just a book about life on Mars and something about serotonin which you and Johnny Lau were talking about the other day.'

'Johnny Lau . . .' Rebecca considered the matter. 'He's mixed up with all this somehow.'

'He was at Christina's party last night,' Joey said, remembering Rebecca tell him that she and Colette had spotted him briefly chatting to Morgan. 'Let's go and see him,' Joey suggested.

'No, first we see Axford,' she said. 'We need the closed-circuit video tapes to use as evidence against Morgan and her gang.'

Rebecca looked curiously at Joey. There was a troubled look on his face. 'What's up?' she asked him.

'There was a locked door leading down to the cellar,' he said slowly. 'I tried to open it.'

'And what did you find?'

'I couldn't open the door.'

'You didn't try and "zap" the lock mechanism?' Rebecca asked.

'Sure, I did,' Joey said. His headache was getting worse now. 'I couldn't. And one other thing, Rebecca . . .'

'What's that?'

'I *hated* you down there,' he confessed. 'I thought

you were scum – just like Yvonne and Johnny and all the others. For a moment, you were *unlike*, just as Morgan thinks you are. Rebecca, what's happening to me? What's happening to all of us?'

Dateline: Brentmouth Cottage Hospital;
Thursday 14 January; 11.21.

Ted Skinner woke up groggily and peered through the transparent screen of his oxygen tent. He sighed to himself. The doctors said he would be all right, he remembered them telling him. He was a stubborn old bird, after all, he'd heard the doctor say to his nurse. A few shattered ribs and a punctured lung wouldn't put him out of action for long.

Ted Skinner's students might have thought of him as a frail old man who could only get around with the aid of a cane. But, back in his younger days, he'd fought in the Falklands War and the Gulf War and Northern Ireland, and there had been no way that he was prepared to let a gang of out-and-out racists pick on two defenceless girls and get away with what they had in mind.

He frowned. He'd never seen such violence before at the Institute. The way the whole world was turning out these days worried him. There seemed to be no respect for law and order, no regard for other people. It was all self, self, self. Stab the other man in the back before he stabs you.

He was aware of the door to his room opening and a white-coated figure moving towards his bed. His doctor, he imagined, coming to give him another of those pain-killing injections. He hadn't wanted them but the doctor, a fresh-faced man young enough to be his son, had insisted.

Peering through the oxygen tent, Skinner could see that this doctor wasn't his usual one. He'd probably gone off to get a couple of hours of well-deserved sleep, he thought.

A hand pulled back the sheet of his oxygen tent. Female hands. Skinner looked up into the face of the new doctor. Black hair, tied tightly back. A cruel smile on her face.

'Sweet dreams, Mr Skinner,' Radclyffe said, and plunged the hypodermic needle into the war hero's arm.

It was only when the spasms and convulsions started that Ted Skinner realised that the doctor wasn't a doctor at all.

It was only then that he realised the New Dawn were winning.

Dateline: General Axford's Office;
Thursday 14 January; 12.00.

There was a strange and tense atmosphere in the corridors of the Institute as Rebecca and Joey made their way across the covered walkway to the admin block and to their appointment with General Axford. Nothing concrete, of course. Just a murmuring of discontent as students huddled in tiny groups along the corridors, their eyes darting this way and that, regarding anyone not in their group with narrowed suspicious eyes.

Axford had to be made to see sense, they'd decided. He had done nothing about the racist attack on Johnny Lau. Nor had he done anything about the posters advertising the latest meetings of the Young Afro-Caribbeans, and the Friends of Zhou-zhun which had recently been ripped from the noticeboard, to be replaced by more flyers promoting the New Dawn. But surely he would have to make a move now that a member of his own staff had been attacked?

When they entered his office, they discovered that the General was alone. Eva was nowhere to be seen. That was a plus, Rebecca realised, as the General offered them two seats. Axford could be much more forthcoming and understanding when the indomitable Eva wasn't around. Her gaze was almost hypnotic, even from behind her dark glasses.

Axford consulted some papers on his desk, the daily reports which Eva prepared for him on every aspect of the Institute. He looked up from them and at Rebecca.

'Griff Rhys-Jenkins' demonstration is still going ahead, I see, Miss Storm,' he said. 'Why haven't you done anything to stop it?'

Why was Axford so keen for the missiles to carry on their planned course past the Institute, Rebecca found herself longing to know. Did he – or more probably Eva – have an ulterior motive? And what was it?

'There have been other things on my mind, General,' she said, a little resentfully. 'Mr Skinner was almost killed last night.'

'Local hooligans,' Axford said. 'I've already had a word with the local constabulary.'

'But we know who did it, sir,' Joey said.

'And you think that Eva and I don't?' he asked.

'Huh?' This surprised Joey and he asked the General to continue.

'The Institute is covered at all times by CCTV,' he said. 'Eva is collecting the relevant tapes even now.'

Rebecca and Joey felt deflated. They should have realised that Eva was one step ahead of them, as always. Nevertheless Rebecca continued.

'It was Christina Haack and Calvin Charles and a whole lot of others,' she claimed. 'I'm positive that Morgan Knight was behind it all.'

General Axford appeared shocked. 'Miss Knight?' he said. 'Surely that's impossible. In the short time she's been enrolled here, her father has proved to be one of the Institute's largest benefactors. He's invested money in the new chemistry lab we're planning on building, given us cash for the new improved catering arrangements.'

'Maybe he's just giving you all that money to shut you up,' Joey accused him. His mind felt as though it was on fire again. Why was Axford being so stupid? Why was it that grown-ups were *always* so stupid?

They weren't like him. They were old. They didn't deserve to–

'That is a very serious accusation, Mr Williams,' Axford said angrily.

'Yeah, and beating up on an old guy ain't serious?'

'Mr Skinner will make a full recovery,' Axford reassured him. 'I spoke to the doctors only two hours ago.'

'Well, then he'll be able to tell you who really did it,' Rebecca said, and turned as the door opened and Eva strode into the room. She paid scant attention to Rebecca and Joey, and crossed over to Axford's desk. She was carrying two VHS tapes which she flung down on to the desk in an uncharacteristic fit of anger.

'Eva?' Axford was disturbed by his assistant's outburst. 'What's wrong?'

'The tapes have recorded nothing,' she told him. 'For three hours last night the whole of the security system was down.'

Joey stared suspiciously at Eva. 'Convenient, that,' he said.

Eva and Axford ignored him. 'You checked the systems before you left last night?' Axford asked Eva.

'Of course,' came her curt reply. 'The systems went down at approximately 19.15 last night. They didn't come back until nearly 22.00 hours.'

A quarter past seven, thought Rebecca, *the same time that Liv's Apple Mac crashed*. And Joey remembered Marc's trouble with his own PC at that time as well.

'What caused it?' the General asked.

'Whatever it was, it was directed right at the Institute,' she said.

'That isn't possible,' Rebecca interjected. 'Nothing could be that precise.'

Eva ignored her and went over to the window, which looked out to the north-east. She could see the lights of the Fetch Hill radio-telescope in the distance. It seemed that she was about to say something when the telephone on her desk rang. She went over and picked it up, and scowled when the person on the other line identified himself.

'No, we have no comment to make,' she snarled angrily and slammed down the receiver.

'Trouble?' asked Joey with a grin. Trouble for Eva usually meant nothing but good for him and Rebecca. Eva ignored him too.

'That was the local press,' she informed Axford. 'They wanted a statement about the attack on Skinner last night.'

Axford glowered. 'I expressly told the police not to release any details to the Press,' he told her.

'Someone has,' she continued. 'And what is more, Skinner has died.'

'Oh no!' gasped Rebecca. She felt terrible. How could she ever forget that Skinner had lost his life on account of her and Colette.

'A weak and ineffective teacher,' Eva said. 'It's probably better that he's gone.'

'You callous cow,' Joey said, and stood up out of his chair. His mind was blazing not just with a headache but with hatred now.

'You know what this means, don't you?' she said to General Axford. 'Media attention will be focused on the Institute. You realise the consequences as well as I do.'

'I do,' Axford said. 'We must act quickly.'

'Listen, you two, a guy's just died here!' Joey said. He'd only met Skinner briefly but he'd always liked the old man. What was more he'd died as a direct result of his trying to save Rebecca and Colette. That made him a hero in his eyes.

'He is of no importance anymore,' said Eva.

That did it for Joey. He ran up to Eva and lashed out at her, kicked savagely at her shins. Eva staggered back – more in surprise than in pain – and then reached out for Joey.

Rebecca darted up and out of her chair and dragged Joey away from the blonde woman just in time. She knew how strong Eva was. She wouldn't have been surprised if she couldn't have crushed Joey's wrists with just one squeeze of her powerful hands.

'Get out of here!' cried General Axford. 'You children, get out of my office now!'

Rebecca and Joey didn't need to be told twice. Rebecca grabbed Joey's hand and dragged him out of the office. Before they left, they took one final look at Eva.

They would have expected her to be seething with anger. Instead, her normally pale complexion was even whiter than usual.

Joey had done the unthinkable. He had done what no one else at the Institute had ever had the nerve – or just the plain stupidity – to do before. He had actually gone and physically assaulted Eva.

Things were getting even more seriously out of control.

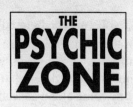

THE PSYCHIC ZONE

7

Take-over

Dateline: General Axford's Office;
Thursday 14 January; 19.13.

'Joey, I'm not sure that I like this too much,' Colette said. Together with Joey and Griff, she was crouched behind the long sofa and potted palm which stood in the corridor outside General Axford's office.

'You want to find out what's going on around here, don't you?' he whispered.

'Of course I do,' she said. 'I met Mr Skinner a couple of times. He was a sweet old man.'

'I'm sure Eva's got something to do with it,' Joey said. 'Those tapes being erased was all a little too convenient.'

'So what do we do?' asked Griff.

Joey looked curiously at Griff. There was something

which was wasn't quite right about Colette's dreadlocked, nose-ringed friend. He wondered what it was. Griff had been at Fiveways when Joey had called around and, when he'd heard of Joey's plan, he had insisted that he come along as well. If Axford and Eva were so keen on preventing his protest, even to the point of threatening Rebecca with expulsion, then he wanted to know why, he said. Joey supposed that he did have a point.

'Axford and Eva always leave the office around about seven o'clock,' he told Griff. 'We wait until they pack up for the night and then we can go and have a sneak around the office.'

'They'll lock the office door,' Griff pointed out.

'Cracking locks is one of Joey's specialities,' she said, and giggled.

'That's where you come in, Colette,' Joey said.

'I don't understand,' she said.

'I tried the whole "zapping" bit at Morgan's this morning on some kind of electronic lock which led down to her cellar,' he told her. 'Zilch.'

'You couldn't work out the numbers?' This sounded serious. Joey could normally turn his psychic powers on and off like water from a tap.

'No, you're going to have to do it for me,' he told her.

'Hey, wait a minute,' Griff said. 'Now *I* don't understand. What's with all this "zapping" business?'

'Leave it, Griff, you'll just have to trust us,' said Joey.

'No,' Griff said firmly. 'You're going to have to trust

me. You and I, Joey, we're two of a kind. We belong together.'

'What about me?' pouted Colette.

'Yeah,' Griff said off-handedly. 'You as well.'

'Joey's got certain powers,' Colette said. 'So have I, but not to the same degree.'

'Certain powers? What kind of certain powers?'

'Telepathy, ESP, psychometry, that kind of thing,' she said.

'Sssh!' Joey said, and told them both to dive down for cover, as the door to Axford's office clicked open and Axford and Eva came out. They paused for a moment as Eva operated the six-digit code on the keypad which activated the door's locking mechanism.

'Is everything organised, Eva?' they heard General Axford ask his assistant.

'If the Press do come then they will discover nothing,' she told him. She reached for the light switch and dimmed the lights, plunging the corridor into semi-darkness. 'The Institute is safe . . .' She hesitated a moment. 'There is one thing that does concern me though.'

'And that is?'

'The Williams brat assaulting me,' she said. 'And the Storm child's story of an attack on Lau Teng Lee.'

'What do you suspect?'

Eva thought for a moment. 'I'm not sure,' she said. 'I will know more later. I have work to do . . .'

'Very well, Eva,' General Axford said. He started to wheel himself down the corridor and towards the exit.

Eva stayed by the door for a moment and then walked off in the opposite direction.

Joey, Colette, and Griff waited for half-a-minute and then came out from their hiding-place. Colette went straight for the door and started to study the electronic lock.

'Hurry up, Colette,' Joey urged, as he cast his eyes up and down the darkened and empty corridor. 'Someone could come along at any minute.'

'I'm trying!' she said, as she tried to probe the mechanism with her mind, searching out the six digits which would give them access to General Axford's office.

'Too late!' said Griff. From down the corridor they could hear the distinctive buzzing of Axford's wheelchair. He had obviously forgotten something and was returning to get it.

'Eva?' Axford's voice echoed down the dark corridor. 'Is that you?'

The sound of Axford's wheelchair drew closer. There was no time to hide. Joey, Colette and Griff raced off in the direction which Eva had taken.

Dateline: Study Bedroom A313, the Institute;
Thursday 14 January; 21.13.

Marc and Rebecca marched down the corridor towards Johnny Lau's study bedroom. He was involved in all this somehow and it was time to confront him. They needed some answers.

Why had General Axford been taking such a keen interest in him – even going so far as to give him biology lessons – when all he seemed to be getting were straight Ds and Es in his essays? What was all that equipment doing in his room?

He had mentioned some family trouble at home. What had that been about? And why had he been associating with Morgan Knight at Christina's party when it was now crystal clear – to Rebecca at least – that Morgan and Christine too were racists of the worst kind?

'You've really no proof for that,' Marc said, as they approached Johnny's room.

'You mean you're not believing me now?' Rebecca asked.

What was it with Marc? Why was he behaving so erratically? Had it really been him who had thrown the firebomb into Johnny's room? And why weren't he and Joey speaking to each other at the moment? She'd quizzed him on that last one earlier, after she'd hung up the phone on Joey when he'd refused to speak to Marc. All Marc had done was to shrug his shoulders and change the subject.

'No,' he said. 'What Christina said to you was terrible. I mean, you can't help being Jewish.'

That stopped Rebecca dead in her tracks. 'What did you just say?'

'Sorry,' Marc said, and the tone of his voice suggested to Rebecca that he didn't feel sorry at all. 'I didn't mean it to sound like that. But I'm sure Morgan isn't as bad as you make her out to be.'

'You don't know the half of it, buster!' Rebecca said, and approached Johnny's room. It was ajar. She rapped on the door. 'Johnny? Are you in there?'

There was no reply. Cautiously she pushed the door open. The room was in darkness and she flipped on the light switch.

Rebecca half-expected a racist comment to have been daubed on the wall just as it had been on Liv Farrar's. To her relief it wasn't.

However, the room was empty. Apart from an unmade bed and an empty desk there was no evidence that Johnny Lau had ever been there. The oriental screen had gone, along with the hi-tech equipment. Even Johnny's shelves had been cleared of his unread books. She rattled the drawer of his desk: it was empty.

'He's left,' Marc said.

'And we know who with.'

'We do?'

'Smell.'

'What?'

'Can't you smell something in the air?' she asked.

Marc shook his head. It was difficult to detect anything when he'd just stuffed his stomach full of a beef curry in the school canteen, he told her.

Rebecca, however, instantly recognised the crisp perfume which lingered in the air. Eva had been here. And quite recently too.

'We have to find her,' she determined.

'How? She'll have packed in for the night now.'

'We'll try the office first, anyway,' Rebecca said, and then stopped. She could hear a noise coming from outside. She went to the window and opened it and looked out.

There was a fight going on in the courtyard below. Two gangs of students were having an all-out battle. Vicious punches were being exchanged. Stones were being thrown. Someone had torn off the branch of a nearby tree and had set fire to it and was waving it menacingly about.

Marc joined Rebeecca at the window. 'Wow, that's some major grief down there,' he said almost approvingly, and grinned.

'We have to stop it!' Rebecca said. She watched on in horror as two boys from the Sixth Form picked on a boy half their size and kicked him to the ground.

Suddenly the fighting stopped. Someone had spotted Rebecca and Marc staring down at them from the open window.

'Unlike!' he cried out. 'Cast out the unlike!'

All their differences forgotten now, the two rival gangs joined in a chant. *Unlike! Unlike! Unlike! Cast out the unlike!*

They charged towards the entrance of the boys' hostel, baying like savages for blood.

THE ENEMY WITHIN

Dateline: The Institute;
Thursday 14 January; 21.30.

Eva marched swiftly down the darkened corridors of the admin block, her feet clacking on the parquet floor and her perfume leaving a crisp and lingering scent in the air. Outside, the moon shone in through the large high windows on one side of the corridor, casting an eerie glow on the old panelled wall opposite. The branches of the yew trees outside tapped gently on the panes of glass.

Eva could hear angry cries and the sound of fighting from far-off. She wasn't worried for herself: she was more than capable of defending herself against any blood-crazed student. In fact, she was almost looking forward to it.

What Eva was concerned about was the sudden breakdown of order at the Institute. The Institute had been planned and designed to run like a well-oiled machine, turning out the world's future technocrats and men and women of power. Something different – something *unlike* – was not welcomed in Eva's perfectly ordered and passionless world.

She paused. She thought she could hear footsteps behind her. And then she heard the smashing of a window in the distance. She couldn't tell whether it was a window in the admin block or in the nearby main building. She quickened her pace.

Behind her, Joey, Colette and Griff emerged from where they had been hiding in the shadows.

'Sheesh, I thought she was going to spot us this time,' Joey whispered.

'Where's she going?' Colette asked.

'Dunno,' said Griff. 'I've never been in this part of the Institute before.'

'You must have been,' Colette said. Griff shook his head.

'Institute students only ever get to go to Axford's office and maybe the staff-room sometimes,' he told her. 'The rest of the building is out-of-bounds. A guy in my year – Jeff Green – was caught snooping around here about twelve months ago. Got himself expelled for his trouble.'

'I heard about that,' said Colette, who had met Jeff once or twice. He'd come down to the village on Sundays to do some gardening work on her dad's estate to earn himself a few quid to supplement his grant. 'Didn't he die in some sort of terrible accident a couple of weeks after he'd left?'

'That's right,' Griff replied.

'From the state of things, no one else has been here for a long time either,' Joey said. He looked around the dark corridor. Paintings, covered with dust, hung on the wood-panelled walls. The curtains draped over the windows were ragged and torn. He went over and tried one of the several old, oaken doors which lined the inside wall. It was locked.

'Come on, let's follow her,' Griff said, and stalked off down the corridor in pursuit of Eva.

Several minutes later, the route they were following took a sharp left and then ended in a dead end. Eva was nowhere to be seen. At the far end of the corridor there stood an old grandfather clock, its tick-tick-tocking the only sound.

'What's it doing here?' asked Colette. She reached out a hand to touch the casing of the clock. Unlike the paintings and the wood panels, the clock was free of dust. The time on its round face read twelve o'clock, midnight. It was either running slow or fast.

'Look, let's get out of here,' Griff said, suddenly.

'Why?' Joey asked suspiciously. 'You were so keen to see where Eva's gone.'

'Look, we've obviously lost her,' Griff said. 'We must have taken a wrong turning somewhere, or she went through one of those doors back there.'

'I don't think so,' Colette said. She stared up at the face of the clock. Twelve midnight.

The sound of fighting was louder now. That decided Griff.

'Look. you two can do what you want,' he said, 'but I'm getting out of here.'

'No, Griff, stay,' said Colette.

Griff took one final look at Colette and then up at the face of the grandfather clock. He murmured his apologies and ran back down the way they had come.

Joey watched him go. 'I guess he's right,' Joey said. 'Maybe we did take a wrong turning. We should get back too. I don't like that noise coming from outside.'

'You can't get any sort of fix on where Eva might have gone?'

'No.'

'Your psychic powers must be really weak,' said Colette.

'Don't remind me,' Joey said. He'd been trying to get rid of his headache for days now. Maybe that was what was screwing him up so much.

'Look at the clock face,' Colette said, and Joey did as he was told.

'So?'

'It's reading midnight,' she told him. 'And we've been standing here for – what? Two or three minutes and it hasn't moved.'

'So it's stopped.'

'Then why is it still ticking?' Colette said.

She reached out and pulled open the grandfather clock's wooden front panel to reveal, not the expected pendulum, but a secret entrance set into the wall behind the bogus clock.

Green light streamed out of the entrance. They could hear the buzzing and whirring and clicking of a thousand computers and surveillance machines. They turned to each other, grim realisation on both their faces. They knew what they had stumbled across, almost by accident.

'The Project,' Joey said.

THE ENEMY WITHIN

Dateline: General Axford's Office;
Thursday 14 January; 21.44.

Marc and Rebecca had escaped from the boys' hostel, just in time. As soon as they had left, the mob of maddened students had hurtled around the corner of the building, foaming at the mouth, their eyes blazing with hatred, determined to rend the unlike limb from limb. Calvin Charles was among them, as were Kevin and Andrew and Christina Haack, all calling out for slaughter. There was no sign of Morgan Knight.

Marc and Rebecca raced across the grounds of the Institute, Marc keeping a tight – too tight – hold on Rebecca's wrist, as they stumbled towards the main Institute building. At least they might be able to find some sort of safety there.

They had no such luck. Another gang was waiting for them there. They turned and ran towards the admin block as a massive explosion ripped the air. Rebecca turned around. The second floor chemistry lab was ablaze. Someone had set fire to the supplies contained there. If it wasn't checked soon, then the whole building would be set alight.

They crashed through the double doors of the admin block and frantically looked for something to barricade the doors shut. Several staff lockers lined the wall and they pushed these in front of the doors. They wouldn't hold their pursuers back for long but it might give them some time. Already they could hear their fists pounding on the doors, soon which would almost certainly give under their constant battering.

'Where to now?' asked Marc, panting and trying to catch his breath. His face looked strained and frightened, but there was still a weirdly ecstatic gleam in his eyes.

'General Axford's office,' Rebecca said.

'What for?'

'We can phone for help,' she said.

'But all the phones are down,' Marc said. 'You told me that.'

'Axford has his own private system that isn't connected to any of the main switchboards,' Rebecca said, and started racing off down the corridor.

'But how do we get into the office?' Marc said. Joey and Colette might be able to crack the code of the locking mechanism, but without a jot of psychic power between them then he and Rebecca wouldn't stand much of a chance.

'We won't need to,' Rebecca said grimly. The door to Axford's office was open. When they stepped inside the office they found that it had been ransacked. Files had been flung over the floor, Eva's PC smashed. A cupboard was in splinters. The phones had been ripped from their connections. On the ground lay General Axford's overturned wheelchair.

'They've got Axford,' Marc realised, and closed the office door. 'Serves the old buzzard right. I never liked him . . .'

Rebecca didn't hear the last comment. 'I don't understand,' she said. And then she froze. The battering noise at the entrance to the admin block had stopped. That could only mean one of two things. Either the mob had given up their chase, or they had broken down the doors.

She heard the pounding of feet running down the corridor. She felt her heart beating loudly in her breast. Would they discover Marc and her here? Would they batter them both to death just as they had poor Mr Skinner?

And then, mercifully, the sound faded off into the distance. Wherever the maddened students were going, it wasn't to this office.

Or was it? The office door creaked open and Rebecca held Marc's arm tightly. There was nothing to save them now. She looked desperately over at the window. It was locked. No place to run. Nowhere to hide. It was the end.

'Griff!'

Rebecca almost collapsed with relief, as she saw the familiar and smiling figure of the Welsh boy come in through the door. She relaxed her grip on Marc's arm. Marc reached out and pulled her hand back.

Something was wrong, Rebecca realised. Marc was holding her tightly. So tightly that it hurt. She looked up into her best friend's eyes.

She looked up into the eyes of a savage.

Then she turned her gaze to Griff. Saw the fire axe in his hand; the axe he'd taken from the fire station at the entrance to the admin block. Griff smiled at her.

'You're not one of us, Rebecca,' he said. He

advanced towards her and raised the fire axe high in the air.

'Don't be stupid!' Rebecca said, and struggled in Marc's arms. No use.

'You're not *like* us, Rebecca,' Griff continued, stepping closer and closer, ready to swing the axe down and cleave her skull in two.

'Yeah, you're *unlike*,' Marc agreed. Saliva dribbled down from the corners of his mouth, as he drooled like a rabid dog.

'And we all know what we do with the *unlike*, don't we, Marcy boy?' Griff said.

''Course we do,' Marc chuckled. 'We cast them out, that's what we do.'

Griff raised the axe over Rebecca's head.

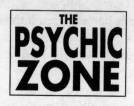

THE PSYCHIC ZONE

8

A Bargain of Necessity

'It *is* the Project isn't it?' Colette gasped, as she stared up at the massive banks of computers that dominated the circular chamber, their myriad lights flashing and glittering in the green-tinged semi-darkness. 'I recognise it from last time.'

Colette had been here before, or at the very least somewhere very similar. That subterranean base had been located under the ruins of the old abbey. It was there that Joey had been held prisoner when she, Rebecca and Marc had first met him. They thought that it had all been destroyed. Now it was obvious that parts of it had survived the cataclysmic explosion of the deadly Mindfire weapon.

Gigantic monitor screens hung from the high

ceiling, displaying images from locations around the world – from the pyramids of Egypt to the rainforests of Brazil. Translucent pipes encircled the walls, pulsating with weird multi-coloured lights. A smaller bank of monitors showed pictures of the Institute.

'Look at this – do you know what these are?' Joey asked Colette, as he showed her another collection of hi-tech instruments. Colette said she didn't.

'It's the stuff Rebecca and I found in Johnny Lau's room,' he told her.

'Johnny is working for the Project?'

'He must be. That would explain why Axford was taking such an interest in him.'

Joey looked around for Eva. There seemed to be no sign of her. There was a series of twelve doors set into the walls at regular intervals. One of them was left ajar. He crossed over to it and peered carefully into the room beyond, prepared to run if he should spot Eva in there.

'Will you get a look at this?' he asked, and let out a loud whistle of appreciation.

'Ssssh!' Colette said. 'Eva could be anywhere around here.'

'Do you see her?' Joey asked.

Colette agreed that the chamber seemed to be empty. If Eva had indeed come here then it looked as though she had left. Eva seemed to be expert at that; disappearing and reappearing as effortlessly and mysteriously as a ghost. She wondered how she managed it.

'Now, come and take a look!' said Joey.

Colette did as Joey instructed her to. What she saw horrified her.

'That's terrible,' she said.

'Terrible?' Joey seemed taken aback by Colette's reaction. 'It's wicked!'

Beyond the door was a room about the size of a small office. One of the walls was stacked high with what looked like missiles. In another corner were piled large canisters, each of them stamped with the mark of a grinning skull-and-crossbones. Even Colette knew that meant that the metal drums contained quantities of deadly poison.

Completely covering the remaining two walls there hung guns and weapons of every conceivable description. There were Colt 45s, which Joey recognised from his time on the streets of Harlem, and hunting rifles and sub-machine-guns which he and Colette had only ever seen in the movies. There were even old-fashioned maces and crossbows, sabres and cutlasses, plus some weapons the likes of which they had never set eyes on before.

'It's sick . . . obscene,' Colette said. She tried to close the door. Joey stopped her.

'It's an arsenal, that's what it is!' he realised.

'It stinks of death,' said Colette, who hated killing and violence of all kinds.

'You could do some pretty serious damage with any of these,' Joey said, with an excited gleam in his eyes. He took a step inside the arsenal. Colette held him back.

'No.'

Joey shrugged her off. 'What's with you, Colette?' he asked. 'Don't you realise what fun we could have with some of these?'

'Killing people?' she asked. 'Is that your idea of fun?'

'Yeah,' Joey grinned, and then stopped as he realised what he was saying. 'No . . . I mean . . . yes . . . I mean . . .' He cried out in pain, shrugged himself free of Colette and brought his hands up to his temples. 'My head hurts!'

Colette reached out for Joey. 'You OK?'

'Of course not,' Joey said. He staggered out of the room and Colette slammed the door shut behind him.

'We have to get you to a doctor,' she said. 'We have to find out why you keep getting these headaches.'

'It feels like when my psychic powers were first developing,' he said, as the headache subsided slightly. 'And now I can't do anything. I can't even read your mind. You think I'm losing them?'

'I don't know,' Colette said, truthfully.

Joey looked back with horror at the closed arsenal door. 'I really got excited in there, y'know,' he said. 'I wanted to take one of them guns and blast everything away. Shoot that racist pig, Marc, and Johnny Lau too, and . . . and . . .'

'What's happening to you, Joey?' Colette asked.

'He's doing what comes naturally, that's all.'

Colette looked over to the grandfather clock entrance through which they had come. Morgan Knight was standing there and, behind her, a gang of about ten students. Some of them were carrying broken bottles or flick-knives. All of them carried an air of murder about them.

Colette stepped away, until she felt the cold steel of the arsenal door against her back. 'What do you mean?' she asked. 'What have you done to Joey?'

'He's letting the savage in his mind take him over,' Morgan said simply. 'Just as all my friends here have.'

'I don't understand . . .'

'That's because you're not like us, my dear,' Morgan said. 'You're different. And we don't like different.' She chuckled. 'We don't like unlike.'

'*Unlike . . . unlike . . . unlike . . .*' the gang started chanting. '*Cast out the unlike . . .*'

'Do it, Joey,' Morgan said. 'You know you want to. I don't know why you've been fighting it for so long. Kill her. Kill her. Kill the unlike.'

Joey turned and looked strangely at Colette. There was no longer any feeling in his eyes for her. Now there was only pure hatred. Colette was different, he told himself. She was wrong.

Unlike.

So she had to be killed.

Dateline: General Axford's Office; Thursday 14 January; 21.54.

A beam of white light shot out and knocked the axe out of Griff's hand just as it was about to split open Rebecca's skull.

Griff yelped with pain and turned to face his attacker as another beam of light hit him full-square in the chest. He fell to the floor and didn't move.

Marc snarled and sprang towards the attacker. A third blast of energy hit him and he too slammed down on to the ground.

'You've killed them,' Rebecca said, as she recognised the person standing in the doorway. She prepared herself for the fatal shot she knew would surely come in her direction.

'Don't be stupid, child,' said Eva, as she came into the room and shut the door behind her. 'The plasma gun was set to stun only.'

'Stun?' asked Rebecca. She watched as Eva replaced the futuristic-looking energy weapon into the inside pocket of her jacket.

'Of course. They'll be unconscious for a while.'

'Why?'

'Don't think I wouldn't kill them if I needed to,' Eva said. 'For the moment they serve my purposes far better alive than dead. Just as you do.'

Rebecca backed away from Eva, not sure what she was talking about, and only knowing that it was bound to be something terrible.

'What do you mean?'

For a second Eva didn't reply. Instead she took in the devastation that had been visited on the office. No flicker of expression crossed her face, neither regret nor anger. She stepped over the bodies of Marc and Griff and reached down and righted General Axford's vacant wheelchair. Then she finally looked at Rebecca.

'I need your help, Storm.'

'I'll never help the likes of you,' Rebecca said. 'I'll see you in hell first.'

'If that is your wish,' Eva replied, and reached inside her jacket for her gun.

'What do you want me to do?'

Eva smiled. 'I'm glad that you're finally seeing reason, Storm,' she said.

'I'll never help you and General Axford.'

'I am not asking you to help the General,' Eva said.

Rebecca was surprised at Eva's lack of concern for the fate of the man who was supposedly her boss, if only in name.

'The General is safe,' Eva said.

'Of course.'

'But I thought that he'd been attacked.' Rebecca said. She looked about the shattered office.

'That is what people such as yourselves were supposed to think,' Eva said, superiorly.

'Well, I won't help your Project either,' Rebecca said. 'Whatever it is. You're evil.'

If Eva was surprised that Rebecca knew of the Project and of her links with it, then she showed no surprise.

'But will you save the Institute?' Eva asked, and then added, almost as an afterthought: 'and perhaps your planet as well?'

'I don't understand.' *Your planet*, Eva had said. Not *our planet* . . .

'Morgan Knight was given a place at the Institute for two reasons only,' Eva said.

'Her father's a billionaire who's donating tons of money to the school.'

'That is one reason, yes.'

'And the other?'

'That doesn't concern you now.'

Rebecca chose not to push the question. She knew that Eva would answer when and if she was ready.

'We thought we could control her, but she is turning more than half the school into mindless savages, interested only in destruction and in obeying her will.'

Rebecca looked down at Griff, the pacifist, who had been ready to kill her with the fire axe. And then at her best friend, Marc, who had somehow been transformed into a racist. Eva nodded, as though reading Rebecca's mind.

'Hatred for the unlike,' she said. 'The most common form of hatred. It was clever of the Knight child to manipulate so basic a sentiment as that.'

'But how?'

'That is for *us* to find out, Storm,' Eva said, and told Rebecca to help her load Marc's limp body into General Axford's wheelchair.

'You said that I could help to save the Institute and the world,' Rebecca reminded her, as she propped Marc up in the chair.

'The Institute was set up with the express purpose of forming and educating the great minds and talents that will rule your planet in years to come.'

'Yes, I know that,' said Rebecca.

Once again: *your* planet.

'And it is succeeding,' Eva continued, even though

little of this was news to Rebecca.

Already several Institute graduates were blazing meteoric trails in the sciences. One ex-student, only ten years older than Rebecca, had just won the Nobel Prize. Several others were high-flyers in the UK's newly-formed Ministry of Technocratic Planning and Development. The company set up by a former computer studies student was threatening to usurp International Electromatix's position as the world's major web site provider; and *The Economist* was confidently predicting in its pages that, within the next ten years, the leaders of the USA, India, Korea and Japan would all have once studied at the Institute.

'But if Knight is allowed to continue her wanton destruction then she will destroy the Institute that we have struggled so hard to build up,' Eva said. 'Already one of the chemistry labs is ablaze. That is only the beginning.'

'You don't sound overly concerned,' Rebecca said, and wondered where they were going to take Marc in the wheelchair.

'Emotion is a waste of time and energy,' she stated. 'But I cannot let her go ahead.'

'And what about saving the world?' asked Rebecca.

'A convoy of nuclear missiles will be passing by the Institute at 04.30 hours precisely tomorrow morning, *en route* for dumping at Penwyn-Mar,' Eva said.

'The convoy which you were so keen on,' Rebecca remembered. She looked down at Griff. With him out of action it looked like the proposed demonstration wouldn't go ahead, after all.

'A public demonstration would have brought unwelcome media attention to the Institute,' Eva said. 'The General and I did not wish that.'

Rebecca decided not to ask the reason behind that decision.

'It is no coincidence that Knight has infected the student population at this precise time,' Eva continued. 'Imagine what would happen if those missiles were to be captured and one of them detonated.'

'Half the country would probably go up in flames – not to mention the Institute and Morgan herself,' Rebecca realised.

'Knight is not concerned with her own survival,' Eva said. 'Morgan Knight has not been Morgan Knight for over six months now.'

'What do you mean?' Rebecca asked.

Eva hesitated before replying and chose her words carefully. 'Let us say, for the moment, that she has undergone what you might call a personality change.'

'Liv told me that the Morgan she knew was a kind and gentle girl – shy even,' Rebecca said. 'No one could change their personality that quickly. What do you mean by saying that Morgan isn't Morgan?'

Eva chose not to answer. 'We have more urgent things to discuss,' she said sharply. 'The missiles come from Zhou-zhun.'

'I've heard of that country,' Rebecca said, remembering the newscast Johnny Lau had been watching when she and Marc had dropped in on him.

'If the missiles were to be stolen or detonated, suspicion would naturally fall on the Chinese Republic from whose territory Zhou-zhun seceded two years ago.'

'I get it. Zhou-zhun's allies – which include the UK and the USA – would blame China; China would blame everyone else. And pretty soon, there'd be global nuclear war. There'd be nothing left alive on the planet within days.'

'You are right except on one point, Storm,' Eva said. '*Something* would be alive on planet Earth. The alien parasite that has taken over the body and mind of Morgan Knight and the bodies of all those others at the Institute!'

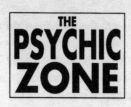

THE PSYCHIC ZONE

9

Dawn of Doom

Dateline: The Project;
Thursday 14 January; 22.15.

Morgan Knight had opened the Project's arsenal and taken out a medieval mace and handed it to Joey. She had decided that it would amuse her and her followers to see Joey smash open Colette's skull with the spiked war-club. The other weapons she would use when they hijacked the nuclear missiles in the morning.

It had been a stroke of good luck that Griff had spotted the grandfather clock clue which led to the Project entrance, just as Colette had done. When Griff had gone back to report to her, Morgan had rubbed her hands with glee. The arms she had stored at Fetch House were nothing compared to the weapons she knew the Project would possess. It would make her task so much easier, she had thought with a smile.

'Kill her, Joey,' Morgan urged. Joey approached the cowering figure of Colette, the mace held in his two hands. 'Cast her out. She is unlike. Cast her out.'

'Unlike,' Joey repeated. 'Cast out.'

His words were coming out in grunts now. He was reverting to savagery, the very same savagery that Colette had seen in Marc and Griff. Why had it affected them and not her and Rebecca, Colette wondered, even as Joey was now almost within striking distance.

She glanced around for something – anything – with which to defend herself. There was nothing.

Joey struck out viciously. Colette dodged, missing the blow by little more than an inch. Joey's mace made contact with a monitor, which exploded in a shower of sparks and flames. The monitor had been display-ing a picture of the Institute's infirmary, but the sick students who were staying there were of no interest to Morgan. She told Joey to continue.

Cast out the unlike! Cast out the unlike! Cast out the unlike! The gang of students chanted, led on by Christina Haack.

The same chant had been heard down through the centuries, although the words had been different. *Gas the Jews!* they might have called out in another time and another place. *String up the niggers! Hang the queers!* The words were different but the sentiments, the hatred and – above all – the fear of the unlike were just the same.

Cast out the unlike!

Joey made another lunge at Colette. Again he missed, but this time Colette tripped and stumbled on a loose-lying length of cable. She fell and smashed her head against one of the pieces of equipment which had come from Johnny Lau's room.

'Now, Joey!' cried out Morgan. 'Kill the unlike!'

Colette struggled to stay conscious. There were no weapons which she could use to defend herself.

No! There was one! She stared deep into Joey's eyes, looked deep into Joey's mind the way she had done with Marc and Griff.

No, Joey, she thought soothingly, trying hard not to transmit to him any of her own fear and distress. *Peace, peace . . .*

For a moment it seemed that she was succeeding, as Joey paused.

And then Colette squirmed in agony as shafts of red-hot pain seared through her brain. It was a headache, but a headache a thousand times more terrible than any she had ever experienced before. It was Joey's headache that she was sharing. Colette didn't realise it but Joey had been possessed by a virus, or evil spirit, or devil – or whatever it was. He had been fighting it with all the powers he had, trying to hold it at bay, trying to stop it from taking over his mind just as it had Marc and Griff and all the other kids at the Institute.

That was why Joey had been in pain for days now. That was why he hadn't been able to call his psychic powers into action. They had all been used up in trying to fight off this possession, just as a healthy body uses all its strength to shake off a physical infection.

But together they could defeat this evil. Together they could expel and exorcise the demon of hatred from Joey's mind.

Colette concentrated, concentrated as she had never concentrated before, concentrated until she thought that her mind would burst.

Out evil! In good! she repeated over and over to herself, reaching out to the psychic zone within Joey's consciousness and breathing in and out in time with her thoughts.

Come on, Joey, say it with me. Out evil! In good! Out evil! In good!

'Kill! Cast out the unlike!'

Out evil! In good! Out–

'Cast out the un – . . . cast out . . . cast . . .

Out evil! In good! Out evil! In good!

'Cast out – cast – cast – cast *Out evil! In good! Out evil! In good!*'

With a final angry snarl, Joey threw the mace at a bank of equipment. As he did so he felt hands roughly grab him by the shoulders.

'We kill him now?' asked Calvin Charles. 'We cast them both out?'

'Yes!' agreed Christina Haack. 'We cast them out now!'

'*No*,' growled Morgan. 'First we find Johnny Lau if we can. As a hostage he is more valuable than they are.'

Johnny Lau? Colette and Joey both looked at each other. What had Johnny Lau to do with all this?

'And then,' Morgan continued.

'Yes?' asked Christina, whose eyes were already blazing with the prospect of violence.

'And then you may cast out the unlike in any manner you choose!'

Dateline: The Institute Infirmary;
Thursday 14 January; 23.12.

Eva never failed to surprise her, Rebecca had to admit begrudgingly, as she helped the older woman trundle the still-unconscious Marc into the Institute's very own on-site infirmary. She had been expecting a dangerous trip across the Institute grounds from General Axford's office, with the possibility of meeting any number of blood-hungry students on the way.

Eva had merely called her a 'stupid child', and walked over to the far corner of Axford's office where she had operated a hidden control in the skirting board. A section of the wall had swung open to reveal the entrance to a secret passage.

Eva had sneered at Rebecca's surprise. For what other reason did she think that she and Axford had chosen to house the admin block in the coldest and most ramshackle building on the site, she had asked her. The whole place was riddled with such passageways, she had told her, the consequence of it being part of the old country house whose family at the time hid priests during the Reformation. Rebecca had nodded. That had been the way Eva always seemed to appear and re-appear apparently from out of nowhere!

The tunnel down which they now pushed Marc was dark and grimy, and illuminated only by a flashlight which Eva had thought to bring with her. It was hot and stifling too, and Rebecca remembered the tunnels she had walked down when she, Marc and Colette had been exploring the ruins of the old abbey. They had nearly caved in on her, she recalled. She looked up apprehensively at the ceiling which was supported by cast-iron buttresses. Eva, it seemed, thought of everything.

Halfway in and the tunnel split up into three different branches. Eva chose the left-hand one and soon they were passing through yet another concealed door into the ground floor of the Institute infirmary.

Their sudden and unexpected appearance was much to the consternation of the patients there, dressed in their nightclothes and dressing gowns. There were about thirty of them in all, boys and girls, all looking weak and underfed: the Institute didn't believe in pampering its patients.

One of them was Liv Farrar, who had been sent there shortly after she had broken down in the matron's office after discovering the racist graffiti in her room. She pointed out the barricaded door to Rebecca, as Eva ordered one of the patients off his bed and man-handled Marc on to it.

'We saw them from out of the window,' she told Rebecca. 'We spotted them attacking some of the other students. We thought that they'd come for us.'

'And they didn't?'

'No, I don't know why.'

'They probably didn't think you were worth bothering about,' Rebecca guessed. 'The weak and the infirm are always the last to go.'

She looked out of the window at the Institute in the distance. Flames were licking around it now. It seemed that the fire in the chemistry labs had caught hold. Even at this distance, she could hear the jeers and taunts of the student mob as they set on yet another unsuspecting and innocent victim.

'Has anyone else been infected in here?' Eva demanded of Liv, as she strapped Marc's arm down to the bed, and produced a hypodermic from the bedside cupboard.

Liv looked at Rebecca. 'Can she be trusted?' she asked.

Rebecca nodded uncertainly. 'For the moment I think so,' she replied.

'No,' Liv replied.

'And Nurse Clare?' Eva asked, referring to the woman who ran the Infirmary.

'We don't know,' Liv said. 'She'd already gone back to the Institute when the mobs started fighting.'

'So you barricaded yourselves in and her out,' Eva said.

'We never thought of that,' Liv said, guiltily. In fact, she and her fellow patients had thought of nothing else.

'It was well done,' Eva said, and injected the hypodermic into Marc's arm and pressed down. 'Survival of the fittest. She was a weak-minded woman whom the General should have dismissed a long time ago. If she dies then she only has herself to blame.'

Rebecca strode over to Eva. 'I don't like your attitude,' she said.

'Are you defying me as well, Storm?' Eva said. 'Like Joseph Williams did? Are you infected as well?'

'No,' Rebecca said. She looked down at the hypodermic which Eva had plunged into Marc's arm.

'What does it look like?' Eva snapped back. 'I am taking a sample of his blood. Before we can fight whatever it is that has taken over half of the school then we must isolate and identify it.'

'You think it's biological?' she asked.

'Yes,' Eva replied. She handed the hypodermic phial with Marc's blood to Rebecca. 'There is a small laboratory upstairs, which Clare uses for routine blood tests,' she told her. 'Examine the blood.'

'But what for?'

'Anything which shouldn't be there, of course!' she said. 'And one other thing, Storm.'

'Yes?'

'I would work very quickly if I were you. Knight and her followers will have discovered the control chamber by now.'

'The control chamber?'

'In the admin block,' Eva explained. 'That will give her access to every part of the Institute. Soon no one will be able to get in or out of the complex. Soon we will all be under siege.'

Dateline: The Project;
Friday 15 January; 00.22.

Morgan Knight looked on with genuine appreciation at the bank of equipment in front of her and flexed her fingers like a conductor preparing to conduct a grand orchestra. Joey and Colette, who were tied up together in a corner, watched her warily. Occasionally Calvin Charles or Christina Haack would come up and spit on them. They were *unlike*, after all. That was all they deserved.

'So, this is how Eva keeps her eyes and ears on every part of the Institute,' Morgan said to herself. 'Hidden instruments watching each and every corner of her accursed school.'

'It's not her school,' said Calvin, who had come up to join her.

'It might as well be,' Morgan said. 'I've known of Eva for years.'

'You have?' he asked, and even Joey and Colette pricked up their ears at this piece of news.

'She was involved in the first *Deimos* spacelaunch,' Morgan said. 'The one which sent Annie Ward into space.'

'I remember,' Calvin said, who always followed news of the latest space launches in *New Scientist*.

'Didn't something go wrong with that launch?'

'It had to be aborted early,' Morgan said. 'I remember Dad telling me about it. The ship ran into some sort of cosmic dust cloud.'

'Cosmic dust?'

'It doesn't matter,' Morgan said, and turned her gaze back to the equipment in front of her. 'Radclyffe and myself were able to shut down the Institute's power and communications equipment briefly from Fetch House. We had our own jamming equipment there.'

Joey turned to Colette. That was what must have been hidden in the locked cellar of Fetch House.

Morgan saw Joey's look of realisation in the reflection of the monitors. She nodded her head. 'We were able to draw power by using the Fetch Hill radio-telescope, near Fetch House,' she told him. 'And then channel it through the radio-telescope into the Institute itself.'

'How?' Calvin wanted to know.

'My father is a multi-millionaire. I can afford many things,' she said.

'How did he make his money?' Colette asked. Like Rebecca, even she knew that an astronaut's salary didn't amount to that much.

'One of his colleagues inherited a fortune when her grandfather died,' Morgan said.

'Annie Ward?' asked Calvin.

Morgan nodded. 'Or as you might know her, my housekeeper, Miss Radclyffe,' she said. 'Prof Henderson was more than happy to let a former astronaut use the radio-telescope to look at the heavens – he didn't know what she really was doing.'

'An astronaut?' Colette could hardly believe what she was hearing. What was a former astronaut doing working as a housekeeper in a sleepy village like Brentmouth?

'And what was the fortune in?' Calvin asked.

'Catering,' Morgan said, and started to laugh. She turned to the others. 'You want to see blood?' she asked them.

'Yes,' they all said, as one.

'And cast out the *unlike*?'

'Yes! *Cast out the unlike! Cast out the unlike! Cast out the unlike . . .*'

'Then it begins now!' Morgan said. She turned back and activated the controls on Eva's command console, the controls which regulated everything at the Institute.

One by one, all the lights in the Institute buildings went out, until the only illumination came from the burning chemistry lab.

The huge iron gates at the entrance to the Institute slammed shut. The barbed wire which lined the perimeter walls started to crackle and sparkle with enough electricity to burn a grown man to a crisp. Every single computer terminal went down. Every phone went dead.

The Institute was now cut off from the rest of the world. The Institute was now ready for the New Dawn.

Only a few hours away a military convoy was

heading towards the Institute, carrying its deadly cargo of nuclear missiles.

The world was only a few hours away from annihilation.

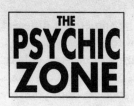

THE PSYCHIC ZONE

10

Casting Out

Dateline: The Institute Infirmary;
Friday 15 January; 03.00.

Eva shone her torch down on the microscope through which Rebecca was studying a sample of Marc's blood. Rebecca looked up and shook her head.

'I'm sorry, Eva,' she said. 'There's nothing unusual in Marc's blood.'

'There must be,' Eva insisted.

'Look, why can't you examine the sample we took?' That question had been nagging on her mind ever since Eva had brought her here.

'I am not . . . familiar with his blood type,' Eva said unconvincingly.

'If I had an electron microscope then maybe I could find something,' Rebecca said. 'But with all the power gone this is the best that I can do.'

'There *must* be something different,' Eva repeated. She reached out for Rebecca's arm.

'Hey, what are you doing?' Rebecca asked.

'*You* haven't been infected!' Eva said. 'You must find what is so special about your own blood.'

'Leave her alone,' said Liv Farrar, who had been standing by and watching Rebecca at work. 'Why haven't you been infected either? Let's take a look at *your* blood.'

Eva shook her head.

'Why not?' Rebecca wasn't going to be cowed by Eva now.

'My blood is not . . . similar . . . to yours,' she said, choosing her words even more carefully than she had before.

Rebecca shuddered in the half-light. She had often joked to Marc and the others that sometimes Eva didn't appear to be human. Had she been right all along?

'So if what has affected Price and the others isn't present in the blood then where else could it be located?' Eva wondered, half to herself.

'What are you suggesting?' Rebecca said and added sarcastically: 'that I should maybe go and take a brain fluid sample off him?'

'Don't be crazy,' Liv said. 'Even if the Infirmary was equipped for something like that, in these primitive conditions, without electricity, Marc would die.'

'That would be no great loss,' Eva said, and stroked her chin thoughtfully in the dark. 'The Price boy was never the finest of students. He would never have fitted in with our grand design . . .'

'You callous–' Rebecca began, and then stopped herself. Something was nagging at the back of her mind. *The brain.* Something about the brain.

'What is it, Storm?' asked Eva. 'Anything might help.'

'Serotonin!' Rebecca remembered. 'The chemical that causes mood swings in the brain. Joey found a book on that and other neurotransmitters in Morgan Knight's room at Fetch House!'

'That could explain why the students have turned aggressive,' Eva said. There was no mistaking the excitement showing in her voice now.

'Not all students,' Liv pointed out. 'The people here at the Infirmary aren't infected.'

'That's hardly surprising with the food Nurse Clare feeds you here,' quipped Rebecca. She'd been sent to the Infirmary once with a bad case of glandular fever. During that time she'd been fed for a whole week on nothing but vegetable soup and carrot juice. That had started to become awesomely boring, even for a committed veggie like her.

That was it!

'I'm a vegetarian,' Rebecca said excitedly. 'Marc, Griff and all the others, they're each and every one of them meat-eaters!'

'You mean, the meat they're serving in the school canteen is infected?' Liv asked. 'Something like that Mad Cow Disease scare of a while ago?'

'Yes. It would make sense, wouldn't it?'

'I knew old Ma Chapman should never have left,' Liv said. 'But Colette isn't vegetarian, is she?'

'No, but she's also not an Institute student so she doesn't eat here.' Rebecca looked at Eva. 'My theory is possible, isn't it?'

Eva nodded. 'If that's true, then the matter can easily be remedied,' she said. 'We can halt the source of the infection and there are a whole host of drugs which can restore and raise the serotonin levels in a human body.'

Once again that distinction. The *human* body. Who was Eva exactly, Rebecca wondered.

Still, there were other matters to attend to first. Like stopping a nuclear explosion for one thing. She turned back to Eva. 'You said that there were two reasons why Morgan Knight was enroled at the Institute. One was that her father donated money to the Institute. What was the other?'

Eva considered whether it would be useful telling Rebecca the truth. Finally she had to admit that there was little point in not doing so. Things, after all, had gone too far now.

'Three years ago, the astronaut, Annie Ward, encountered a cloud of cosmic dust on her mission to Mars,' Eva said.

'Cosmic dust? What do you mean? Why did we never hear about it at the time?' asked Rebecca. 'My dad worked at Mission Control then . . . before he died.'

'Ah yes, Nathan Storm,' Eva said.

'You knew him?'

'No,' Eva lied. She smiled. She didn't want the Storm child to know that her long-lost father was really the Project Controller. She would hold that knowledge back from her until the time she chose, until the time when it could cause the greatest damage.

'So why didn't we hear about it at the time?' Liv repeated Rebecca's question.

'It was decided that knowledge of her encounter was not in the public's best interests.'

'Who decided?' Rebecca asked, and then supplied her own answer. 'It was *you*, wasn't it?'

Eva declined to respond to that question. 'When she was examined, it was discovered that her mind had been affected by some sort of alien virus; a mind parasite that fed on her thought waves; a parasite that was, however, not infectious, unless one came into close proximity with it. The crew of the second *Deimos* mission weren't affected, for instance.

'The crew of the third *Deimos* craft, the ship carrying Armstrong Knight, would have passed nowhere near the cloud, if their mission hadn't been delayed by twenty days–'

'I remember reading about that in the Press and seeing it on CNN,' said Liv. Her eyes gaped wide-open with shock. '*You* were responsible for the mission being delayed, weren't you?'

'It was a calculated risk,' Eva said. 'Armstrong Knight became infected and, when he returned to Earth, passed on the infection to his daughter, Morgan Knight, just as had been planned.'

'This second reason for Morgan being admitted to the Institute,' Rebecca persisted with her original line of questioning. 'What was it?'

'Morgan has great telepathic abilities,' Eva said. 'The virus, in itself, isn't harmful to you humans. But feeding off the minds of a telepath such as her, it would amplify her talents, would give her a willpower which few could be able to resist, especially if, as Storm suggests, their serotonin levels are low. In such a case, it would give her the powers of persuasion of a Hitler, or a Genghis Khan, or a Caesar. It was considered that she would prove to be a very valuable weapon for the Project. Or, at least, that was the theory . . .'

'And your theory has proven wrong,' Rebecca realised.

'We–' Eva corrected herself. 'It was considered that the Knight girl and the parasite in her mind would be able to live together in some sort of symbiotic relationship, each of them nourishing and feeding off the other.'

'And they haven't.'

Eva nodded. 'The mind parasite has taken her over completely, feeding off her psychic energies until it has become too powerful,' Eva said. 'And what does any parasite want to do to its host body?'

'It . . . it wants to feed off it and eventually destroy it,' Rebeecca said.

'Precisely, Storm, the parasite wants nothing more than to annihilate the entire human race, until it remains the only living creature on this planet.'

'You're talking about the end of the world,' Liv Farrar realised.

'Yes, I am.'

Rebecca thought hard for a moment. 'And all this is happening because you discovered that Morgan is a telepath?'

'Yes.'

'But we have our very own telepath right here at the Institute!' Rebecca said. 'We have Joey!'

'Williams never came into contact with the parasite when it was infectious,' Eva said. 'Nor will he be of any help to us now. He has been infected by the contaminated meat. His powers will be weak. He will be under Knight's control just like all the others.'

'No,' Rebecca said, and remembered Joey's headaches. 'He's been trying to fight it ever since he became infected. He could be our only chance!'

'Where did you last see the Williams child?'

'He and Colette told me that they were going to break into Axford's office,' Rebecca told her.

Eva controlled the temptation to express her outrage. Instead she remembered the footsteps which she had heard following her down the corridor to the entrance to the Project.

'Then he will have gone to the Project,' she said. 'That is where Morgan Knight will be too.'

'How do we get there?' Rebecca asked. 'Does the tunnel we took lead there as well?'

'No,' Eva said. 'That passage will only take us to the office.'

'Then let's go,' Rebecca said, and then a moaning

sound from the bed made her turn around. Marc was coming round.

'That means the Rhys-Jenkins boy will also be recovering from the effects of the stun blast,' Eva realised. 'Soon he will realise the route we have taken. Soon he will be leading the others down the tunnel.'

'Then we'll have to go across open ground,' determined Rebecca.

'Don't be stupid,' Eva said. 'They'd kill us the moment we set foot outside the infirmary.'

'There's no other way,' said Rebecca. 'Besides, if what you're saying is true, then Morgan's bound to be organising them for an ambush on the nuclear convoy. They're going to be far too busy to notice us.'

'It is dangerous.'

'Yeah, but I'm prepared to give it a go,' Rebecca said, angrily. 'I don't know who you really are, Eva. I don't even know if you're human or not, and quite frankly, right now I don't care. All I'm really concerned about is the fact that this is my planet, and I don't want to see it go up in a ball of fire just because one off your experiments has gotten out of hand. Now, are you coming, or am I going to go it alone!'

Eva looked out of the window, at the fires still leaping out of the chemistry lab and at the crowds of students who were now congregating around the burning building trying to put out the flames. It stood to reason, of course. A fire on-site would only attract attention, which was exactly what Morgan Knight didn't want. That was also what she and General

Axford hadn't wanted, but for different reasons, of course.

In a few hours it would be dawn. It could be the last dawn that the human race would ever see. Eva turned to Rebecca.

'I will go with you, Storm,' she said.

Dateline: The Institute;
Friday 15 January; 04.15.

Dawn had not yet broken, when Rebecca and Eva cautiously left the Institute Infirmary. There was deathly silence in the air, apart from the occasional twittering of some early-rising birds.

Just once or twice they heard some cries of pain and realised that somewhere, someone was being attacked by one of Morgan's blood-hungry followers. The smell of burning hung in the air; the chemistry lab fire had been successfully put out.

It seemed that Rebecca had been right after all, Eva realised as they made their way across the grounds towards the main complex of buildings, keeping always under cover of the yew trees which dotted the grounds. Morgan had organised all her students for the ambush. The nuclear convoy would pass by the main gate: that was where the majority of them would be.

But not all of them. As they approached the shadowy bulk of the main Institute building, a shot burst through the air. Eva cried out and fell to the ground, blood already oozing through the black sleeve of her jacket.

Rebecca reached down to help her to stand. Eva swatted her away as she would a fly. 'I need no help from the likes of you,' she snapped, as she staggered to her feet.

'Look!' Rebecca said, and pointed to the roof of the Institute building. There, silhouetted against the white of the moon, stood Kevin and Andrew. They were both aiming rifles down at them.

Rebecca grabbed Eva's hand and dragged her across the grass as the two rooftop snipers fired on them again. The earth erupted all around them as the bullets thudded into the ground.

Finally they reached the cover of the walkway which connected the main building to their destination, the admin block. Yet they were far from safe.

A blaze of white-hot energy flashed just inches in front of them, shattering the concrete of the walkway. Calvin Charles was standing before the entrance to the admin block, one of the futuristic plasma weapons from the Project's arsenal in his hands.

'Come no further, *unlike*,' he said, his voice guttural and savage. 'The New Dawn must be allowed to come.'

'Don't be stupid, Calvin,' Rebecca said.

'The world must be cleansed in fire,' he said. 'The New Dawn must come.'

'Morgan – or the thing that's taken her over – wants to kill us all!' she said, but there was no reasoning with Calvin.

Eva whipped her own gun out of her jacket and fired on Calvin. He cried out in agony and crashed to the floor, beside the open doors.

'What have you done to him? Stunned him, like the others?'

'Killed him,' was Eva's steady reply as she ran towards the doors. 'Now hurry.'

Rebecca stood in horrified disbelief at Calvin's dead body. She stood too long for her own good. A gang of three students, led by Christina Haack came around the corner.

'Storm! Behind you!' cried Eva.

Eva ran back and fought off the students, bashing them with her good right hand and the butt of her plasma gun. She dragged Rebecca away from them and managed to pull her into the entrance hall, where she slammed the doors shut.

'Thank you,' Rebecca said as she struggled to catch her breath.

'Don't thank me,' Eva said. She reached into her jacket and took out a revolver. She handed it to Rebecca, who refused it. Eva replaced inside her jacket pocket and then made her way down the corridor which led to the Project.

'They might have killed me,' Rebecca said, as she followed Eva, quickening her pace to keep up with her. 'Why did you save me?'

'With you dead, what reason would Joseph Williams have to believe me? Now, hurry! We haven't much time!'

THE ENEMY WITHIN

Dateline: The Project;
Friday 15 January; 04.22.

Morgan Knight – or rather the creature that now possessed Morgan Knight's brain and mind – watched on with scarcely concealed glee at the pictures on the monitor screens before her. Each of them showed a different image of the Institute.

By the closed gates of the Institute, now electrified to prevent any intruders, a small gang of students, armed with Project weapons, was waiting. When the nuclear convoy came within sight, then the gates would open automatically and they would pour out and halt the motorcade.

On the roof of the boys' hostel, the dreadlocked Griff Rhys-Jenkins, now fully recovered from the effects of Eva's weapon, was seated behind what seemed like a bazooka, but which Joey and Colette both knew could easily have the power of several thousand tons of TNT. Occasionally, he glanced back towards the Infirmary. Liv and the others had been locked in there. Once the nuclear missiles had been taken, then he and his mates would have some sport with them.

On another rooftop, Christina Haack was poised behind another similar weapon. Other Institute students hid themselves in the trees lining the route which the convoy would take.

A final screen charted the progress of the convoy on its way to the Institute.

'You won't win, you know,' Colette said futilely, from where she was sitting on the floor of the circular chamber, tight up back-to-back with Joey.

'I already have done,' Morgan said, and smiled at the person who was now entering the room. Colette glared evilly at the figure of Miss Radclyffe, the housekeeper from Fetch House – or rather, Annie Ward, as they now knew her to be.

'Joey defeated your control over him,' Colette said. 'And he defeated the aggressive feelings that you'd put into him. He can defeat you as well.'

'Then why hasn't he?' Radclyffe asked. She took a revolver from out of her pocket and aimed it at the two of them. Even though they were tied up, she was taking no chances.

Joey didn't reply. His headache had gone, now that he had cast out those evil impulses that the combination of Morgan's powers and the infected meat had instilled in him. Now there was a reassuring and familiar tingling in his head. He could feel his powers returning. If only he had enough time to recover. If only. . .

'Stop the ambush now, Knight, or you will die.'

Everyone turned to see Eva and Rebecca enter the room. Eva was aiming her plasma gun at Morgan. Morgan seemed singularly unimpressed and didn't even seem to mind when Rebecca went over to untie Joey and Colette.

Radclyffe watched on too, but didn't fire. *It might be amusing to see what these two brats would try and do*, she thought, sadistically. *Let them think that they might be winning and then shoot them down.*

'Killing me won't solve anything,' Morgan said.

'It will give me a great deal of pleasure,' Eva replied.

'How can you kill something which is in my *mind*?' Morgan asked, and turned back to the screens. Just another half-a-mile and the convoy would be at the Institute gates. Everything was going perfectly according to plan.

Eva lowered her gun slightly. She knew that Morgan was right. Even if she destroyed Morgan's body, that wouldn't destroy the parasite which had lodged in her mind. Through Morgan's psychic domination of the Institute students, a tiny bit of that mental parasite was in their mind as well. They had to expel the parasite from Morgan's mind, before her control would be relaxed. And how do you battle something that is in the mind?

Eva looked over at Joey and Colette, who were now staggering to their feet and rubbing their legs to bring some feeling back into them. She nodded to Rebecca. If anything had to be done, then it had to be done now. Rebecca whispered something to Joey.

Morgan clasped her hands in triumph. The nuclear convoy had reached the final turning in the road. Within a matter of seconds it would be in full view of the Institute. In a matter of a few more seconds, the world would be on its way to nuclear holocaust.

'Morgan, you can't do it,' Joey said, and walked slowly towards her. 'You can't kill an entire planet.'

'Can't do it? That's precisely what I am doing!'

'Morgan Knight wouldn't do it,' he said. He stood still, facing her. Morgan turned around.

'Morgan isn't here,' she said. 'She hasn't been here for a long time. She has been cast out.'

'Oh yes, she is,' Joey continued, trying hard to probe deep within Morgan's psyche, trying to locate the alien mind parasite which had so completely taken her over. 'A little bit of that shy and nervous creature that was Morgan. She's still there You can't erase her completely.'

Morgan frowned a little. She could feel a dull but insistent throbbing in her head.

'*I* defeated it, Morgan,' Joey continued relentlessly, looking hard into Morgan's eyes. 'Fight it. Cast it out. Don't let it steal your soul.'

'I . . . I don't know what you're talking about,' Morgan said. She was lying. She could feel Joey's thought waves crisscrossing with hers. The alien parasite could feel it too.

'Cast it out, Morgan, cast it out!' Joey said, and started to repeat the mantra that Colette had taught him. *Out evil! In good! Out evil! In good! Out evil!*

'Yes,' Morgan said, quietly. 'Out evil! In good! Out . . . No!'

Out evil! In good! Out evil! In good! Still Joey continued. He couldn't fail now.

In the road outside, the driver in the lorry and his police escort noticed some movement in the trees near that fancy private school for posh eggheads. It was probably their imagination, but they slowed down a little all the same.

'No!' Morgan cried out again. 'Cast out the unlike! Cast out the unlike!'

'Out evil! In good!' Joey said. 'Out – yes, out, cast out the unlike.'

Cast out the unlike! Cast out the unlike!

Rebecca looked urgently first at the picture of the nuclear convoy on the monitor and then at Eva.

'He's failing!' she cried. 'He's not strong enough to fight her on his own!'

Colette came forward and grabbed Joey by the hand. She looked into his glazed eyes. 'Joey, try!' she pleaded. 'Together we can do it! Join your mind with mine! Please, Joey, try...'

Joey looked strangely at Colette, as if he couldn't recognise her.

'Cast out the unlike,' he said. 'Cast out–'

'No!' Colette said. *Out evil! In good! Out evil! In good! Cast out – cast – out evil! In good! Out evil! In good!*

'Yes, that's it, Joey! You can do it!'

They both turned to Morgan.

Out evil! In good! Out evil! In good!

Cast out the unlike! Cast out! A change seemed to come over Morgan as she tried to withstand the onslaught of Joey and Colette's combined psychic powers. Her knees buckled under her. She fell to the floor.

Cast out the unlike! Cast out the evil! Cast out the evil! Out evil! In good! Cast out the evil!

She moaned and brought her hands to her face as the demon parasite was finally expelled from her mind. She screamed and screamed and screamed again, and then suddenly she was the old Morgan once more, the shy and retiring girl who never had a bad word to say for anyone.

'Dad! she cried out. 'I want my dad!'

Throughout the Institute, students suddenly came to their senses. They looked aghast at the guns in their hands. They threw them down to the ground in disgust. They rubbed their foreheads, wondering what they were doing in the trees, on the rooftops, outside the gates as a new dawn broke.

Down the road, the nuclear convoy trundled past them, undisturbed.

In the Project, two gunshots filled the air. Joey, Colette and Rebecca saw Morgan slump to the floor, dead. A little way off, Radclyffe also fell to the ground and the revolver which she was holding in her hand clattered onto the metal floor.

Eva replaced her own revolver, the one she had offered Rebecca, into her jacket pocket. She smiled at the three of them.

'I saw Radclyffe aiming at Morgan,' she explained. 'I tried to stop her. I must have been too late.'

Rebecca stared suspiciously at Eva. 'Yeah, I bet,' she said, and went over to Radclyffe's revolver and picked it up. It was stone-cold.

She hadn't been fooled. Eva had killed both of them, rather than have her plans exposed to the authorities.

But she didn't have any proof.

With Eva there never was any proof.

THE
PSYCHIC
ZONE

Epilogue

Incubation

*Dateline: General Axford's Office;
Friday 22 January; 16.15.*

'We failed, Eva,' said General Axford. 'It was a gamble, and a gamble which didn't pay off. A gamble which nearly ended in nuclear war. Which nearly resulted in the death of the Project.'

'Not so,' Eva said, and smiled.

The two of them were sitting on either side of the General's desk in his newly-furnished office. On the desk between them, there stood a small glass jar. Inside it, there was a thick blood-red liquid.

'In fact, the Project Controller is pleased at the

outcome,' she said.

'He is?'

'Of course.' She tapped the glass jar with her fingers thoughtfully.

'Morgan Knight is dead,' he reminded her. 'We will no longer be able to use her psychic energies in the way we had planned.'

'Once the parasite became too strong, she was useless for our purposes,' Eva said.

'There is dissent amongst the students at the Institute,' Axford said.

'And once their serotonin levels have readjusted there will not be,' she stated, confidently. 'The new caterers I have employed will see to that. Some pacifiers in their food will also ensure their future compliance in our plans, just as the drugs in their food lowered their resistance to Morgan Knight's commands.'

General Axford looked concerned for a moment. 'And will it make them forget what happened?'

'Of course,' Eva informed him. 'They will have a few nightmares but that will be all.'

Axford nodded towards the glass jar and its contents. He raised an eyebrow in interest.

'I had Morgan Knight's body exhumed,' Eva said.

'Her father did not mind?'

'Her father met with an "accident".'

'Ah, I see . . .'

'When Morgan first contracted the virus, it had a physical presence in her brain,' Eva explained. 'It was only when it fed on her psychic abilities that it also gained a mental existence and became dangerous.' She indicated the liquid in the jar. 'Contained in there is all that remains of the parasite in its physical form, extracted from the Knight girl's brain itself. We will examine it, develop it, stimulate it, test it on the students at the Institute.

'That is why the Controller of the Project is so pleased with us. Properly controlled and developed, the parasite will enable us to extend the power of the Project over the whole of the planet.'

Axford leant back in his wheelchair and took a deep breath. Sometimes his so-called assistant's audacity and ambition frightened him.

'There are many people who would not like that,' he pointed out to Eva.

'Of course,' she said with a glacial smile. She took off her glasses and stared at General Axford.

The General shuddered, as he recalled the first time he had ever met Eva, back on that visit to Mission Control at the time of the *Deimos I* launch. No one knew where she had come from, but they had all agreed that she was a brilliant, if manipulative, scientist. And ever since that day she had exerted a terrible power over him, just as she had influenced Nathan Storm, who had been in charge in Texas at that time.

Then, the two men had joked that they would have done whatever Eva asked them to do, just as the Institute students had obeyed the commands of Morgan Knight so willingly. Neither of them knew how terribly true their comments would be.

Eva had come to the Institute as his personal assistant, even though it was she who ruled. Ruled him, with an unearthly power. Ruled also Nathan Storm, who thought that he was the Project Controller, even though, in reality, it was Eva who used him as a puppet ruler. For she knew that many of the rank and file of the Project mistrusted her, and even her mental powers could not persuade all of them.

For it wasn't the mind parasite which was the real danger to Earth. The parasite was a danger to Eva and her Project, and that was why it had to be stamped out.

The danger to planet Earth was Eva.

Eva: cold, ruthless, and *inhuman*, who knew that the way to take over a world was not by war or violence, but by stealth and secrecy and cunning and infinite patience. By placing people loyal to her in positions of power. By creating the technocrats and the scientists, the businessmen and the politicians of tomorrow. By influencing the life of each and every Institute student until they served her will, whether knowingly or not.

A few – freethinkers like Storm and Price and Williams and their friend, Russell, – would fall by the wayside. They were not important.

For Eva was but the advance guard of an alien invasion, waiting somewhere out in space, and the likes of which the world could never have dreamt of. And, when Eva judged that the Earth was ready, when the Presidents of all the major countries in the world, of all the major corporations, of all the major computer companies, were in power, then her masters would strike.

'Of what possible interest are the concerns of the Earthlings to us?' Eva said. 'After all, we are superior. We are the Project.

'And what are they? They are nothing. They are but the *unlike* . . .'

Dateline: Junior Common Room, The Institute;
Friday 22 January; 16.17.

Colette entered the Junior Common Room and walked up to Marc, Rebecca and Joey, who were all waiting for her. They had finished for the day and Colette had suggested that they all celebrated the start of the weekend by trying out a new vegetarian restaurant in the nearest town.

No one had protested, not even Marc and Joey. They'd recently lost their taste for meat. And none of them had sampled the food provided by the new caterers either. They knew that Eva would have learnt a lesson from the previous caterers, who had been supplied by Radclyffe. It was a lesson they also knew that she would use to her full and deadly advantage.

She passed Griff and gave him a cheery smile. Griff attempted to reciprocate, but the truth was that he'd been miserable for a week now. He couldn't believe what a prize idiot he'd been, sleeping through the passing of the nuclear convoy. Where were his eco-warrior credentials now, he kept asking himself over and over again.

'No one remembers a thing,' said Rebecca, and Marc nodded. The events of a week ago had been only a hazy recollection in his mind too. It had taken Joey and Colette's combined powers to jog his memory.

'Look, there's Johnny,' Colette said, and she stood up to greet the young Oriental boy. They had thought that he was Chinese. Now they knew differently. She performed a mock curtsey. 'Well, hello, Your Highness,' she said.

'Please, do not remind me of my deception,' he said with a smile. 'It is not in the nature of my people to lie.'

'We would have kept your secret that you were the son of the Emperor of Zhou-zhun,' Joey said. 'Hey, I've never met real-life royalty before, y'know!'

'It was better that only the General Axford knew,' Johnny said.

'And Eva too, I bet,' Rebecca muttered.

'We misjudged you, Johnny,' Marc said. 'We're sorry.'

'Misjudged me?' Johnny asked. 'For what?'

Marc sighed. It seemed that Johnny's memories of the racist attack on him were fading rapidly as well. 'It doesn't matter.'

'It was General Axford who suggested through his contacts in the Ministry of Technocratic and Forward Planning that I stay here at the Institute,' Johnny continued. 'Threats had been made to my father that I might be kidnapped if the missiles passing by the

Institute were not returned to the Chinese Government who considered them still to be their property.'

'And where better to hide you than right in the path of the missiles themselves?' Rebecca said. 'That's why Axford was so keen for Griff's demo not to go ahead. It would have drawn too much attention to the Institute. People say that the Chinese are cunning. They can't hold a candle to Axford and Eva.'

'That's why all the books in your room were unread as well,' Joey realised. 'But what about the hi-tech gizmos?'

'Communications equipment to contact my father wherever he is in the world, together with a book of access codes,' Johnny explained.

'I still don't understand what was in it for General Axford though,' said Colette.

'A brand-new laboratory complex, and an annual payment for the next ten years.'

'Of course. The Institute must come first,' said Marc.

'It always does,' agreed Rebecca.

'I have to go now,' Johnny said. He'd spotted Christina Haack entering the common room looking for him. 'Christina is taking me to Brentmouth tonight. There is an anti-racism concert there.'

'Well, well, well,' said Joey, after Johnny had made his goodbyes and departed. 'And we thought he might have been one of the bad guys!'

'Just goes to show that you can't judge by appearances,' Marc said meaningfully.

'He doesn't even remember where Axford took him

when the mobs started rioting in the grounds,' Colette said.

'Down one of those secret passages, I bet, until Eva sorted the situation out.'

Rebecca sighed with frustration. 'We're the only people who remember what happened!' she said. 'Eva's won again.'

'We've no evidence against her or Axford,' Joey said.

'Calvin Charles is dead,' Colette said. 'You can't deny that.'

'Yeah, killed in an accident in the fire that destroyed the chemistry lab,' Joey said bitterly. 'His body was burnt beyond recognition. Or at least that's the story that Eva's putting about. And the insurance paid out to his folks will sure keep them from asking any awkward questions.'

'We still know where the entrance to the Project is,' Colette pointed out.

'The admin block has been cordoned off,' Rebecca told him. 'It's to be pulled down and replaced by the new labs. Building work's already started. You can bet your bottom dollar that there'll be no evidence of the Project ever having been there, once the contractors Eva has called in have finished.'

'So, you were right, Rebecca,' Colette said, glumly. 'Eva really has won again.'

'For the moment,' Marc said, and collected his things together and stood up to go. 'But one day, she'll make a mistake. One day she'll go just that little bit too far.

'And, when that day comes, all four of us are going to be there. And then, once and for all, we'll expose Eva and Axford and the Project for who they really are!'

THE PSYCHIC ZONE

Mathew Stone

Read the first three chilling books:

The Institute is a school for brilliant young scientists, but even Marc, Rebecca, Joey and Colette can't explain away some weird and sinister events . . .

Book 1: Mindfire

A ball of flames sets part of the Institute on fire, but this is no accident. For clearly burnt into the ground is the eerie outline of a fox. Could this be anything to do with an ancient curse laid on the old Abbey – where the Institute now stands . . ?

Book 2: Changelings

A plane crashes, but there are no bodies found. Meanwhile, people are mysteriously disappearing on Darkfell Rise, and a comet is coming ever closer to Earth. Could there be a link with all these events and Colette's strange new friends . . ?

Book 3: Alien Sea

The gang's holiday in Cornwall is interrupted by the discovery of a micro-circuit by a group of archaeologists digging for ancient relics of King Arthur. And now one of the diggers is having nightmares! But when the gang ask questions, they're threatened by some nasty thugs. Who wants this discovery kept a secret?

Paranormal? Or a cover up? The truth lies in the psychic zone . . .

THE PSYCHIC ZONE

Mathew Stone

0 340 69836 5	MINDFIRE	£3.99
0 340 69840 3	CHANGELINGS	£3.99
0 340 69841 1	ALIEN SEA	£3.99

All Hodder Children's books are available at your local bookshop or can be ordered direct from the publisher. Just tick the titles you would like and complete the details below. Prices and availability are subject to change without prior notice.

Please enclose a cheque or postal order made payable to *Bookpoint Ltd*, and send to: Hodder Children's Books, 39 Milton Park, Abingdon, OXON OX14 4TD, UK.
Email Address: orders@bookpoint.co.uk

If you would prefer to pay by credit card, our call centre team would be delighted to take your order by telephone. Our direct line *01235 400414* (lines open 9.00 am–6.00 pm Monday to Saturday, 24 hour message answering service). Alternatively you can send a fax on *01235 400454*

TITLE		FIRST NAME		SURNAME	

ADDRESS	

DAYTIME TEL:		POST CODE	

Signature ....

Expiry Date: ....

If you would NOT like to receive further information on our products please tick the box. ☐